CW01460201

AFFLICTION Z: FRACTURED (PART 1)

BOOK 4 IN THE AFFLICTION Z SERIES

L.T. RYAN

LIQUID MIND MEDIA

Affliction Z: Fractured (Part 1)

Copyright © 2018 by L.T. Ryan and Liquid Mind Media, LLC. All rights reserved. No part of this publication may be copied, reproduced in any format, by any means, electronic or otherwise, without prior consent from the copyright owner and publisher of this book. This is a work of fiction. All characters, names, places and events are the product of the author's imagination or used fictitiously. For information contact:

Feedback on this book can be sent to:
Ltryan70@gmail.com

Or on the web:
http://LTRyan.com
http://www.afflictionz.com
http://www.facebook.com/AfflictionZSeries

ONE

Thousands of shards of tiny icicles pelted the remaining leaves and snow-covered ground. The freezing rain added a slick coat to the six inches of powder present from the morning's snowfall. The setting sun's rays failed to penetrate the heavy cloud cover. As night fell, temperatures would plummet and traveling would become even trickier for Sean Ryder. It was hard enough to traverse icy terrain with two good legs, let alone one.

He'd repaired or replaced his makeshift prosthetic almost daily since leaving the cabin in North Carolina. It had snapped on him a few times, once when a group of afflicted were in pursuit. Marley instinctively knew Sean was in trouble and led them away, carrying on with his barking and quick movements through the woods. It was a full day later when the dog returned to Sean's side.

They were now four weeks into a two-week journey. The weather had turned in the past ten days and temperatures had fallen, reaching the twenties overnight. It happened much sooner than Sean had anticipated. He couldn't recall the last time he'd seen snow in early November in Virginia. He was prepared to make the journey south in such weather, *after* he reached the bunker, found his prosthetic, and resupplied himself.

Keep pounding.

He'd heard the mantra a decade earlier from a Panther's football player. It repeated constantly in his mind. There were times it was the only thought in his head. Of course, at other times he thought of all he had lost. And in the worst of times, he recalled his final moments with Kathy, and he feared what had become of Emma. His daughter was in good hands with Turk. If she was still with him. That was another reason he had to reach the bunker. He had to contact Turk and the others in the network.

The last time he'd seen his property it wasn't in good shape. The bunker had been breached and damaged. He held out hope that it wasn't so severe he couldn't at least repair the comms equipment enough to make contact.

Sean faced west, leaned back against a tree and closed his eyes. He imagined the sun, big and bright as it crested a far-off mountaintop. The warmth coated his face, chest, arms and legs. He breathed in deep. The icy air cut at his lungs and the mental facade crumbled. The weather was bound to turn again. After all, he was in Virginia. Next week it'd probably be in the eighties.

"Just hang in there," he muttered to himself.

Marley looked up at him, head cocked slightly to the side. Sean removed his glove and reached down to pet the dog. He worked his fingers through Marley's thick fur, past the damp layer and into the warmth.

"You're a lucky bastard, you know that?"

The dog seemed to smile up at him as he panted, perhaps waiting for Sean to flip him a hunk of the jerky he'd found in one of the houses they'd scavenged along the way.

Lucky bastard indeed.

He reached into his coat pocket and pulled out a quarter-full sixteen ounce bottle of water. He drank it in two swallows. Before putting the bottle away, he bent over and packed it with snow.

The atmosphere changed in that moment. It felt dense and the air grew still. Marley's ears perked. He whimpered softly. The constant plinking of ice pelting the ground faded into the dreaded sound of shuffling.

Sean straightened, leaned back against the tree and armed himself. In his left hand he held a Glock 19 loaded with seven rounds. It was his last resort since gunshots would draw more of the dead to his position. In his right hand he held a machete with a twenty-inch blade. The tip and sharp side were stained dark red with the decrepit blood of the afflicted.

The first wails cut through the muted sounds of their steps. They sensed he was near. The woods made it difficult to tell which direction they were coming from. Were they on a collision course, or would they pass by? Sean watched Marley. The dog honed in on the location of the dead. Through the falling sleet and snow Sean made out their shapes. They were no further than a hundred feet out and passing by. He counted twelve but knew there were more based on the noise level.

He gripped the machete tight, ready to attack. Playing the role of the passive survivor was against his nature. He used to parachute into hostile areas from thirty thousand feet armed only with a pistol. Killing these damn things wouldn't be an issue, especially since none he had seen so far had the ability to move quickly like some of the afflicted he had encountered years ago in the Nigerian facility.

The tail end of the group passed through the woods thirty feet from his position. Marley crouched low in the snow, ears back, ready to pounce should one get too close. Sean remained ready for the stragglers.

The shrill wails continued from further ahead in the herd. One of the last called back. How far ranging was this method of...*communication*? Christ, would they one day all be drawn together in the middle of the country? Wouldn't that be one hell of a rager. Let the Mississippi swallow them up.

A few of the dead appeared to get snagged along the way. Shielding his eyes from the snow, Sean noticed they had encountered a fallen tree in their path and were unable to get past. The world would be a better place with at least a few less of the afflicted wandering it. Sean started moving slowly through the snow. His makeshift prosthetic cut a line in the accumulation. He was easily trackable, but there was little he could do about it.

He approached the afflicted from behind, circling wide to make sure he hadn't missed any others. He took refuge behind an old oak that must've seen the forest's death and rebirth a couple hundred times. Three afflicted stood in front of the fallen tree. One had impaled itself through the gut on a broken branch. The brainless bastard had continued all the way to the trunk.

Sean shoved the pistol in an oversized coat pocket and made his approach. The putrid smell hit him at ten feet out. It hadn't been that long since he'd last encountered it, but the odor always hit hard. He fought back against the choking cough building up in his throat. The machete sliced through the air, back over his shoulder, then down, splitting a younger man's head in half.

He pulled the blade back, pivoted on his good leg, planted his prosthetic firmly into the ground, then lunged forward, swiping the weapon from the side and hitting the second afflicted in the forehead before it had a chance to react. She stood there for a moment, eyes dulling as the last embers of life faded. Her body collapsed to the ground in a thick pool of dark blood.

The final afflicted looked back at Sean while continuing to push forward against the tree trunk, unsure how to free itself.

Sean took a moment to catch his breath. Turned out to be a moment too long.

The afflicted began wailing, sending out a long, high-pitched shriek that sent a flock of crows rising from the skeletal remains of a cedar. The sky above turned dark with their numbers. The swoosh of their wings overpowered the sound of falling snow and ice. The calls rang out, at first the birds, and then the afflicted. Their yells to each other echoed through the woods.

"Shit!" Sean lunged forward and swung the blade hard, hitting the dead man at mid-ear and lopping off the top of his head. It collapsed forward, bent in half at the waist.

Barking arose from behind him.

Sean swung around. "Marley!"

The dog ran toward him, alert, his head swinging left to right and back. He refused to settle down.

"Let's go, boy." Sean began moving north, perpendicular to the direction of the horde. If anything, a few might return from the group. More concerning were the smaller bands in the woods who might now be drawn to the death cry of the last afflicted.

The forest surrounding them hummed with activity. The afflicted called out from all directions. Signaling to one another? Trying to locate each other? Sean had encountered similar activity over the past four weeks. Was the need to group up a side effect, or one of the last remaining shreds of humanity in the afflicted mind?

They moved slowly through the woods. Sean kept his head on a swivel, always looking for signs of the dead. Through the wails he heard a different sound. More human. He glanced down and saw that Marley noticed too. The dog stood with his head cocked, staring off to their left. Sean leaned over, placed his hand on the back of the dog's neck and scratched there.

"What is it, boy?"

Marley opened and closed his mouth a couple times, each time letting out an almost nonexistent whimper.

Then Sean heard the sound again. There was no doubt it was from a living human.

"Help!"

He zeroed in on the direction Marley's nose pointed. He proceeded tree to tree, constantly looking over his shoulder for signs of being trailed. It wasn't only the afflicted he feared now. Where there were humans, there was an ever-increasing chance of being taken prisoner, made a slave, or used as bait for the dead. It was close to the point where Sean almost preferred the afflicted. At least they were predictable in their behavior.

It was the living you had to exercise the most caution around.

The cry for help grew closer. Sounded more desperate. Marley moved a few feet ahead.

"Stay with me, buddy." Sean pulled the pistol from his coat. He racked the slide and chambered a round. He cared little of what lay in his path, and kept the barrel pointed directly in front of him.

He heard the groans before he saw anything. The guttural sounds indicated death was imminent for someone. Based on the cracking of bones, it had already come for at least one person.

Sean made a fist and held it out. Marley stopped and crouched toward the ground. Sean looked back, nodded, and hoped that the dog would stay put for a few minutes.

"Please," a woman said. "Please don't hurt my baby."

There were groans and grunting in response to her plea.

Sean inched around a tree. He spotted two of the dead feeding on a man. One tore into the flesh of his upper leg, while the other was face down in the gut. The man somehow clung to life. His eyes darted wildly. His mouth was twisted open, but nothing other than a hollow sound emerged. His gaze settled on Sean for a moment and he managed to lift his arm and extend a single finger. Sean eased his head around the tree.

Fifteen feet away another man struggled with a third afflicted. Blood coated his arm but it was impossible to tell if he'd been bitten. There were more dead scattered on the ground. The trio had managed to take several out before being overwhelmed. In the distance, another small group of dead approached.

On the ground a woman clutched at her lower leg. She looked around frantically. Tears streamed down her face. Sean recalled her mentioning her baby. Where was the child? Had a fourth member of their party taken it? Or a group of people they had encountered? Surely an afflicted would simply kill the little human and eat it where it fell.

Sean took a deep breath and then emerged from behind the tree. He moved quickly toward the struggling man and drove his blade into the back of the afflicted's head. It slid in and out as though it were made of butter. The being collapsed on top of the guy. Sean turned his attention toward the woman on the ground.

"Are you hurt?" he asked.

"Th-th-those two over there. Save my husband, please."

Sean looked over his shoulder. The lights had gone out for the man now. He knew the two afflicted would pose no danger for several minutes, but he couldn't make the woman watch as her husband was devoured. He made his way over and dispatched two of the dead. A quick glance back with a shake of his head told the woman that her spouse had not survived. As she buried her face in her hands, he severed the man's head to ensure that he would not come back to life.

"Your baby," Sean said, walking back toward the woman. "Where is it?"

The man on the ground had worked his way out from under the weight of his attacker. He crawled over to the woman, put one arm around her shoulders, and the other over her abdomen. Sean noticed it then. She was pregnant.

Very pregnant.

"Jesus," he said, wiping sweat from his face and glancing back at the remains of her husband. "What happened to you guys?"

The man struggled to get to his feet. His legs were wobbly. He looked around the area. He reached down for the woman and helped her up. "They're getting close. Help me with her and I'll tell you along the way."

Sean hesitated for a moment. He was armed. They weren't. At least that he could tell. On the one hand, he had an advantage. On the other, he had something they might want.

"Please, man," the guy said. "She's in shock. I can't carry her on my own right now."

Sean noticed the wound to the guy's shoulder. "That's going to be bad."

He lowered his gaze to the ground. "I know, and I'll deal with it soon enough. I gotta get them to safety."

"Where's that?" He studied the man for a moment.

The guy held his hand out. "Help us."

Sean slid the machete into its sheath and shifted the pistol to his right hand. He threaded his left arm around the woman and they began to move away from the scene.

"Why are you out here?" Sean said. "And where are you headed?"

"There's a group not too far from here," he said. "I came upon them while scavenging. They welcomed us to join, so I went back to the house we were holed up in and convinced my brother it was best. This place, it has a doctor, food, walls, weapons. They're surviving in this crazy world."

Sean couldn't help but think of the places like that he'd encountered so far. Things were never as they seemed. Every fiber of his being told him to stop right there. So he did.

"What are you doing?" the guy said, glancing over nervously. "They're getting closer to us."

"I'm not—"

The woman screamed. Her knees went weak and the men nearly dropped her.

"What is it?" the guy asked her, frantically searching her body for a wound.

She pulled her arm free and grabbed her stomach. "The baby's coming."

TWO

"IT'S TIME." TURK SAT BELOW DECK WITH HIS GROUP, PREPARED TO break the news. "We've collected everything we could. We have enough gas to get us into the Bahamas. And we've picked up enough extra people that we have good numbers now."

Faces filled with anticipation stared back at him. His wife Elana and daughter Layla, holding hands. Emma Ryder, Addison Bowen, and the two girls who'd journey with them, Jennie and young Paige. Paige and Layla had become friends over the past several weeks. And Sarah, who enjoyed watching the young girls. Finally, there was Rhea. The woman could handle herself in any situation, and Turk was glad to have her around.

And there were newcomers who had joined them only recently. A family of seasoned fighters. The father had been a Marine. His wife and two teenage sons were well trained. Definitely an asset to the group. Turk would be lying if the large canisters of gasoline in their possession hadn't swung him in favor of bringing them along.

And then there was the lone man he'd found drifting in a

lifeboat shortly after they found the ship. Turned out the guy had been a police officer.

These were the kind of people he needed fighting by his side to keep his family safe.

Turk continued. "We're going to leave tonight." He scanned the faces staring back at him. Emma had tears in her eyes. Turk offered a comforting smile, but doubted it did any good. Part of the reason he'd kept them anchored for so long was the hope that Emma's father would radio in. Sean Ryder had survived that Nigerian hellhole. Helped Turk get out of it, too. Then Sean lived through a government coverup. Sons of bitches made the guy think he was crazy. He deserved to reach the promised land.

But it was time, and Turk knew it.

"The trip won't take but a few days. Once we reach the island, we'll have everything we need to survive. It's self-sustainable for the most part. There might be occasional scouting trips, mostly to look for wandering survivors, but the majority of you won't ever have to worry about that. We're going to rebuild and make the most of our lives." He rose and stood in front of the stairs, bracing himself against the steady swaying of the boat. "Hell, I don't know about you all, but I'm kinda happy not to have the internet to distract me anymore."

There were a couple chuckles, but everyone knew an easy life was a thing of the past.

Turk took a deep breath, forced a smile, and looked at each person in turn. "We have to make the most of what we have now. And we have to be ready to fight for it. I don't know what lies ahead, but after talking with each one of you about your experiences, and knowing what my own family went through, there are others out there who want what we have, if for no other reason than to say 'fuck you' to us. They might want to take this ship and burn it just to watch us try to swim to shore."

Jerry, the Marine, leaned forward.

"Yeah, Jer?"

"Seen it happen even before this mess," Jerry said. "When lawlessness prevails, the worst in humanity comes out."

"That's right," Turk said. "It does. So let's all be prepared. We have enough weapons and ammunition for everyone, even the little ones." He pointed at his daughter and Paige, whom he had taught to shoot on a couple of Ruger 10/22s. "Nothing will stand in our way."

His wife nodded, followed by Jenny and Alec, the cop stranded on the lifeboat. Soon, everyone in the room joined in.

All except Addison.

Two hours later he stood at the bow, one foot perched on the chrome rail, the other planted on the deck. The sea was calm now. The boat rolled gently. From his position he saw open water to the south and east. He couldn't care less what was behind them as long as it wasn't someone coming for him. To the west the setting sun loomed large over the faint outline of Charleston. The sky was painted red and purple. The air smelled of salt. He'd grown accustomed to the smell. So much so that when he went to town, the initial wave of death odor now gagged him.

So much difference between here and there, he thought while recounting the things he'd been through in Charleston. It got him and his family to this point in time, so there was no reason to regret anything he'd done.

"I'm leaving."

The sound of Addison's voice sent a jolt down his spine. He straightened, pulled his shoulders back and turned to face the woman.

"Is that right?" he said.

"It's time," she said, using his own words against him. "I have to get to my grandparents."

"You have no idea what you'll find when you get there." He wondered if she understood this point. "They could be filleted.

Mutilated. Or worse, turned into one of those...things. Are you prepared to deal with that?"

Addison didn't blink. "With what I've already made it through, I'm ready for anything, Turk. If they're dead, then they're dead. If they're one of those things, I'll put them to rest. I'd rather it be me than some crazed ex-Special Forces guy with a hatchet."

"Hey, I'm one of those crazed ex-Special Forces guys, you know."

She nodded and smiled broadly. "I'm just giving you a hard time."

"Fair enough," he said. "I'm giving you one now."

"I know, and it's not going to dissuade me. If I have to dive over the side of the boat and swim to shore, I will."

He stretched his arms high, clasped his hands and cradled the back of his head. "Once you're gone, you're gone. I can tell you where we're going, but I can't leave you with anything to help you get there. No maps or directions. Can't risk those falling into the wrong hands. You understand that? We'll likely never see each other again."

She crossed her arms and nodded while her eyes misted over. "This is the last time we'll ever be face-to-face. If I make it to the farm, I'm never leaving it."

"*If...* see, you understand how risky this is." He took two steps toward her, reached out and wrapped his hands around her shoulders and squeezed gently. "We're stronger with you, Addy. We need you here. We want you here. Hell, I'll just say it. I want you here. I know how you feel. I really do. I've lost most of my family. I have a daughter out there somewhere, and I'll never know if she survived."

"You want to go on like that?"

He bit down against her stinging words. "No, I don't. But I have to because we have no choice. We gotta do what's right for us right here. See, you're my family now. Jenny, Paige, Emma, all of you. I do everything for you now."

"I appreciate everything you've done, but I have to do this." She pulled free of his grasp and turned away. Her head was surrounded by the deep reds of the setting sun. "I'm sorry."

"I can't force you to stay, and I'm not gonna stop you from leaving. We won't be hanging around, though. The moment your raft is unhitched, we're heading south."

She looked back at him, eyebrows arched. "The raft?"

"Can't expect you to swim two miles to shore in November."

"But what if you need it?"

"We'll find another along the way. Besides, I'm not counting on any more shore expeditions until we get to the island, and that water will be warm enough for me to swim in."

"I don't know what to say."

"You don't have to say anything. I told you, you're family now. I'm not gonna let you go without giving you a fighting chance. Now come on, let's get the boat ready."

They packed her bag with two weeks worth of provisions, so long as she ate light. No problem there. They had all grown accustomed to a single meal a day. Turk opened a lockbox and gave her a Smith and Wesson 9mm pistol, along with an extra magazine and a box of ammunition. He also handed her a knife and a hatchet.

"Try not to use the pistol unless you have open road in front of you."

"I know." She ejected the magazine, checked the barrel and slid the magazine back in. "It draws them in."

"I spotted a horse farm not too far from my old bunker." He laid a map out in front of them and traced a line southwest. "I guess about ten miles. This was early on, so I have no idea if they survived, or if they've already been looted. Worth a look, though.

If you can secure one, it'll cut your travel time to a third of walking, and help you escape any sticky situations."

She nodded.

"Fuel was harder to come by the past two weeks. I imagine that's the case everywhere. Fewer and fewer cars will be on the road."

"Safer, I'd imagine."

"In some ways." He wiped a layer of sweat from his brow and onto his pants. "And like the fuel, the weak are being thinned out. More and more of the people you run into will be the wrong kind. So keep to yourself and don't go looking for anyone, no matter what you hear. Be wary of anyone you come across, no matter how pathetic they look. I wouldn't put it past some to create traps by leaving a child in the middle of the road. They'll shoot you and loot you and not give a single God damn about you."

"I don't doubt it." She removed the hard plastic cap off the hatchet's blade and ran her index finger down it. "You should stop stalling. It's gonna be completely dark soon."

He nodded, smiled, extended his hand. "It's been a pleasure, Addison Bowen."

"Likewise, Turk."

He escorted her to the stern where the raft waited, hovering a few feet over the water. He helped her into it, then lowered it to the water. The line went slack in his hands. He stared into the remnants of the setting sun, watching the raft drift toward the shoreline until darkness had swallowed it whole.

"God speed, Addy." He turned away and headed to the helm. The engines roared to life. He throttled forward and the boat began its journey south. His gaze shifted to the right, toward the faint outline of land. Before long, it had faded.

"It's time."

Each passing minute brought a sea of memories flooding Turk's consciousness. He tried to avoid the thoughts, but there was nothing he could do to stop them. Friends and families, now gone, would be impossible to forget. He had to honor them, and the only way he knew how was to survive.

Help others survive.

Rebuild.

Even if he saw no point to it.

Turk's mind eased after an hour had passed. The cool, steady breeze and gentle sloshing on the rolling waves lulled him into a meditative-like state for the next forty or so minutes.

"She's gone."

His wife placed her hand on his shoulder and pulled him toward her. Her eyes watered over. The wind? Or something worse.

"What?"

"She's gone, Turk."

He glanced away. He'd dreaded this moment. No one else knew Addie was leaving.

"I know," he said, holding eye contact for a moment. "I let her go."

ELANA'S HAND slid off Turk's shoulder and down his chest as she took a step back. A vertical crinkle split her lower forehead as she looked up at him like he was crazy. "Why?"

"She had to find her grandparents. Who was I to tell her she couldn't? Think you could've stopped me if I decided to go after—"

"No, not Addy." Shaking her head, Elana reached out again, one finger raised.

"Then who?"

Tears spilled from her eyes and ran down her soft cheeks. The moonlight glinted off them. "Emma."

"What?" Turk gripped the wheel so hard he thought it might snap in his hands.

"Emma's gone, Turk. We thought she was sleeping. I went to wake her to eat and she wasn't there."

"You've looked everywhere?"

"It's not that big of a boat."

Turk's chin touched his chest as he stared down at the blank space between him and his wife. Emma had stowed away. She knew Addy was leaving and holed herself up on that raft. Addison was old enough and strong enough and had the right mental fortitude to make the journey. But Emma? He knew Sean had taught the girl well, but could she last for a month in the afflicted world?

"She's so young," Elana said, wiping tears away.

He lifted his head and his gaze drifted toward the vast darkness behind them. "We've gotta—"

"No," Elana said. "We don't. What we need to do is take care of the people on this boat. The ones who want you to protect them. Don't damn these souls by turning around for someone who didn't want to be here anymore."

He stared into his wife's wavering eyes for a moment. The look on her face continued to plead for him to take full responsibility for those who wanted to be with them at this moment. And that did not include Emma. He nodded at Elana and turned back to the controls. He kept the wheel steady, and for the rest of the night, they did not divert from their course.

After Elana had left, Turk looked back at the darkness one more time.

"I'm sorry, Sean. I truly am."

THREE

"How far's the camp?" Sean restrained his voice the best he could. There were stragglers all around, but so far none had noticed the trio. Perhaps the smell of decayed flesh from the three afflicted Sean had killed was enough to keep them away.

The man looked up at him. His thick and scraggly beard was a mix of grey and brown. His blue eyes were wide, bloodshot. He had one hand on his sister-in-law's round stomach, the other behind her back.

"About five miles," the guy said.

Sean wanted to collapse on the nearest stump. Five miles? They'd never make it that far. "You said you came from a house. Said it was a good place to hole up, right?"

The guy peered over his shoulder at an encroaching dead. "Uh, yeah, we were there for a few weeks. Never bothered."

"How far away is that?"

The guy was too concerned over that afflicted to have heard Sean.

"Forget about them," Sean said. "I got your back if they come close. Now tell me, how far away is that house?"

The guy swung his gaze back to Sean, stared up at him with a hollow expression as though he were still processing the question.

Sean was close to kicking the guy in the head and taking off with only the woman. Hell, the man had suffered a bite...at least he thought it was a bite. Could've come from being thrown against a branch or something.

"Man, you gotta work with me here. I'm gonna level with you. Five miles, it ain't happening. Not in her current condition. I'm capable of delivering a child. Done it before. But I don't see it going over so well out here." Sean crouched in front of the woman. "She's not gonna be able to keep quiet. And the baby sure as hell isn't. So I need you to tell me right now, where the fuck is that house y'all were holed up in?"

The man blinked Sean back into focus. His head bobbed several times. "Right, yeah, okay. It's hardly a half-mile from here."

"Now you're talking," Sean said. "Come on, help me get her on her feet."

"I can't." The woman stared at her deceased husband. "Just leave me here. If it's meant to be, I'll make it until you return with help."

"Get up, Beth," the guy said.

"I'm sorry, Leo." Her head dropped until her chin hit her chest. "I just can't."

Sean pulled up his pant leg and knocked on the hunk of wood helping hold his body up. "You see this?"

Beth shifted her gaze to the side and focused on his makeshift prosthetic.

"If anyone had an excuse to give up out here, it was me. Sons of bitches took what I had and for weeks I've been hobbling along on whatever branch I could find that'd support me. I got no idea when these'll snap off either. But goddammit, if that happens, I'll crawl my ass to where I gotta go. So Beth, I need you to get your ass off the ground and move. You hear me? Get up!"

The three of them were motionless for a few seconds. Beth's face tightened into a knot, all scrunched toward the middle. She grabbed each man's hand and gripped and squeezed and grunted as she pulled herself off the ground. Her belly pushed out, her butt lifted, she got her knees under her and completed the transition.

"A half-mile," Sean said.

"A half-mile," Leo repeated.

"We proceed cautiously, but we can't just take our time. We need to get out of this forest."

Leo nodded. "Follow my lead, and we'll be there in no time."

They picked their way through the woods, stopping a couple of times for Beth to rest. During these moments, Sean scouted ahead a hundred yards or so with Marley at his side. He dispatched lingering afflicted he found along the way. He noted they were different today. Moving slower, perhaps? Was it the cold? He wasn't sure how that could have an effect. There wasn't any blood flow going on, at least not like in himself or other living beings. Maybe muscle stiffness, for those who still had enough muscle to be affected by it. Whatever, he told himself. No point in worrying about it too much. Another data point to file away until he met someone who could use the information.

After his last jaunt ahead, Sean returned and wiped dank blood off his fingers against the thick bark of an oak. "Path's clear."

Leo rose from a squatting position and took a few steps toward him. He stuck his arm out, his index finger stretched past Sean, bounced up and down.

"It's just over that ridge," he said.

Sean followed Leo's outstretched digit and thought he could make out the shape of a house. Just his mind tricking him. It was tough enough to see fifty feet with the falling snow. It had picked up over the last ten minutes. Was it going to continue to do so? Were they in for a record snowfall for the region? The house better be well stocked.

They helped Beth to her feet and began the slow trudge through the rising snowfall covering the ground. It was at least half a foot now. The flakes coming down were big, fat, and wet. The kind that would keep building off the one that fell before it. There was a time Sean enjoyed it. He knew he never would again.

A gentle lull fell upon them. The afflicted had settled and their wild calls faded into the sound of the wind through the trees, rustling any remaining leaves that clung to the top of the canopy. The snow made its way, little pellets pounding softly.

He thought of Emma. Wondered what she was doing at that moment. Had Turk decided to move on yet? Would they wait for Sean? He knew Turk had a plan. And Turk had to see that plan through. He could not wait for anyone, including Sean. Even if Turk had Sean's flesh and blood under his protection.

Sean had almost made peace with the fact he might never see his daughter. But he always phrased it as so: might. He wasn't ready to throw in the towel completely. He'd made it this far. His house was a few days' travel. He could rest with these folks. See to it that the baby was okay. Then be on his way again. By now, there'd be little to loot from his property. The most important things there wouldn't stick out to most. People figured communication equipment was worthless now, at least anything beyond a walkie-talkie or portable radio. And his leg, well, if someone needed it more than he did, then he figured they should help themselves. It was made for him. To fit him. He doubted anyone who came across it would need it. But that didn't mean they wouldn't take it. Not in this new world. Could be a good bartering chip someday.

"There it is," Leo said.

Sean struggled to see the structure through the whiteout. The other man's pace quickened and Sean had trouble keeping up with the sudden change. His wooden prosthetic got stuck on a root. He couldn't pull it free. Both Sean and Beth fell. Sean managed to twist so that he came down on his side. But Beth wasn't as capable of adjusting. She hit the ground hard on her stomach and let out a loud cry.

He crawled over to her, helped Leo turn her over. She held her stomach tight with both hands. Her face was red, lips drawn tight, eyes clenched shut. Sean saw why right away. She'd landed on a large, jagged-edge rock.

Several seconds passed and the tension on Beth's face eased. Her brother-in-law doted over her, smoothing her hair back, whispering that it was all going to be okay.

Sean got to his feet, turned in a circle to scout the area. Dark figures hovered off to the right. Six of them, maybe more behind.

"We gotta get to that house now," he said.

Leo lurched upright, shook his shoulders out. He reached down and pulled Beth off the ground. He cradled her in both arms and stammered forward, shuffling his large feet through the snow, leaving behind deep tracks anyone could follow. Sean did his best to cover them as he trudged behind. But all he did was make it more obvious they'd been there. Didn't matter, he told himself. There were footprints leading this way for half a mile.

Three sets.

Side by side.

Obvious that one person wasn't able to support themselves entirely.

They climbed the hill, struggling against the wind and snow and the pitch of the ascent. The house came into view below the roofline. It was a simple structure, built square. Four walls and a roof. Couple of windows cut out. They hadn't been broken.

A stretch fifty-feet long of virgin snowfall stood between them and the front door. Every step sent a chill further up Sean's leg. It had even started to affect both legs. Leo stopped next to a tree. He leaned back and let Beth slide to her feet. Her knees buckled. He supported her, helped her back up. Then he stuck his hand in his trousers and pulled out a keychain. The sound of the keys clattering against each other rose above the howl of that frigid wind.

The thing that dashed through the open space between the house and that skeletal tree moved quicker than any of the afflicted Sean had seen since Africa, where all memories were still mired in the desert sand. He could barely yell "look out" before the afflicted was on top of Beth.

Marley reacted before Sean or Leo. He raced across the short distance and plowed headfirst into the dead. The afflicted went sprawling onto its side and sank into eight inches of snow until it settled on the ground. It wriggled, but it seemed that being surrounded as it was affected its speed.

Sean freed the machete from its sheath and hurried over, fighting against the loosening prosthetic fixed to his thigh. He brought the blade high and dropped to his knees. The afflicted let out a gag as Sean lopped off the top of its head.

Leo's hands shook and slid off Beth as he attempted to lift her off the ground. "D-d-did you see that? How fast that sumbitch moved?"

Sean pointed at the house. "Go unlock the door. I got Beth."

Leo found his keyring in the snow and scooped it up. He staggered toward the house, repeating what he had said moments ago.

Sean leaned over and helped Beth to her feet. "I can't carry you, hon. Can you walk the rest of the way?"

She grimaced as she cradled her stomach with both hands. "I think I can do it."

Sean assessed her condition as she started forward. "It didn't get you, right?"

"I'm okay."

"All right. We're almost to a safe place. One foot in front of the other. That a girl." He stayed with her the entire way with Marley a few paces ahead, ears perked up, gaze aimed at some unseen dead in the woods through the white veil that surrounded them.

He stopped underneath the porch, handed Beth over to Leo.

"Come on, boy," he called to Marley. The dog trotted over, sat down next to him. Marley refused to come inside when Sean entered. "Gonna take point for a while?"

Marley looked back out toward the skeletal forest.

Sean closed the door. The floor plan was wide open with a closet and bathroom that he figured wasn't operational at this point. There was a couch and a couple of plastic chairs like he had out on his deck at home. He took off his gloves and cupped his hands and exhaled a hot breath into them. Rubbing them together, he took a closer look at the kitchen and stopped in front of the square window overlooking the back.

He stood there for several minutes, watching the snow fall and the shadows darken as the sun began its trek westward. How had that afflicted moved so fast? He hadn't seen a single one do that since Africa. He'd figured the ones bred with that trait had died in the bombings. That the ones who escaped were slow and dimwitted. Maybe it was recessive, only one in a million or so would have the ability. Another thing to be mindful of, he told himself, all the while hoping he never saw another like that.

Beth cried out. The contractions were getting closer. The baby would come soon.

And he couldn't shake the feeling that something worse was coming with it.

FOUR

ADDISON BOWEN HAD REACHED SHORE AND NAVIGATED INTO THE marshlands. The winds died down. There were no waves. And the dead couldn't reach her there. She dropped anchor and settled in for a long night alone.

When she woke, thin wispy clouds raced past the moon which hung low and reflected off the rippled water. White twinkles of light filled the sky. The first traces of pink lined the eastern horizon.

A fish slapped against the surface then popped out a moment later, splashing hard when it landed. The sequence sent a shiver down Addy's spine. She shone her light across the cove, expecting to see an afflicted trudging toward her. What would happen next? Would it walk all the way out and stand below grasping at the watery space between it and the raft? The light fell upon a section of disturbed water.

"Just a fish," she muttered.

She grabbed the paddle and plunged it below the surface. She'd performed the exercise earlier to make sure she was in at least five feet of water. Again, the paddle failed to reach the bottom.

The silence that followed left her more uneasy. When had nature died? In the previous months, the birds and insects were always present, one giving way to the other with the cycles of the sun. But lately, there was nothing. No crickets, cicadas, blue jays, robins.

Silence prevailed.

In time, she'd adjust. But for now, her intense focus on the quiet meant there'd be no more sleep. It was too early to set out on foot, though. This was the time of the dead. She glanced toward the east. Another finger of light had overtaken the dark horizon. Thirty minutes, she figured, before she'd set out.

Addy unzipped the duffel and looked through the supplies. There was too much. Certainly more than she could carry herself. She had stuffed her backpack with enough to last her two weeks. After that, she'd scavenge. Turk had come through with more. What would be helpful? Food and water, for one. He'd left her with some purifying tablets and a few filter straws. Enough to provide her with four to six months of suitable drinking water. Maybe more if she conserved use.

She also took the stock of energy bars he'd stuck in there. Two boxes of twenty-four. Each bar provided almost two hundred calories. She could survive two weeks on the supply alone. Best to save it for the end, she figured. She could scavenge and hunt early. The energy and drive were there. A month from now that might not be the case as she battled winter in the mountains.

Would it take that long, she wondered? A month to reach her grandparents? It all depended on how much of the journey she had to take on foot. If Turk was correct, and that horse farm had been untouched, she could reach it by afternoon. Ten miles. With a healthy steed the distance would be easier to manage. She wouldn't push the animal. Twenty miles a day was plenty, and would get her to Charlotte inside three weeks, and that included any possible delays that could, or more likely would, arise.

When Addy finished going through the duffel, she had one knife clipped to her belt and two more hidden in her boots. She had a Glock 19 9mm pistol concealed behind her back, and a Glock 17 on her waist band opposite the knife. Turk had also supplied her with a spare magazine for each, and a box of 9mm rounds. She hoped she wouldn't need to break into them, but that was wishful thinking, and she knew it.

The tip of the sun now crested the skyline. The water around her rippled in orange and red and pink through the rising steam. She breathed in the salty, clean air, filling her lungs deep. The temperature hadn't changed, but her cheeks warmed with the light. She tugged the opening of her right glove with her left index finger and exhaled into it, then repeated the sequence on the other side.

Inspiration filled her soul at that moment. She could do this. No, she was destined to do this. Her grandparents were on their farm, fortified and thriving with a community. That's who they were. That's who they would continue to be.

Addy pulled the anchor hand over hand until the twenty-pound dumbbell cleared the water with a thick sucking and slurping sound. She heaved it into the boat on a pile of blankets that she hadn't needed overnight.

"Ow!"

Addison nearly fell backward over the inflated railing. The tips of her fingers plunged into the frigid water. Her feet scraped on the bottom of the raft, but there was no where for her to retreat to.

The blankets moved up and down, side to side. A small hand appeared out of the far end. It grabbed the edge and began to pull it down.

Addy tugged the Glock 19 out of the holster clipped to her waist and struggled to get a hold of it with both hands. She

L.T. RYAN

lowered her hands to her waist. Steadied herself. Wouldn't do her any good if she fumbled the pistol overboard. Besides, what exactly was she looking at?

The thick gray blanket wrinkled as it lowered. Emma's pale face and blue eyes appeared with the ever-rising sun surrounding her like a halo.

"Emma?" Addison unthreaded her shaking finger from the trigger guard. "I could have shot you."

That was the only thought going through her head at the moment. But it wasn't the only question she had.

Emma's lip trembled. "Please don't make me go back, Addy. I've got to find my father."

The life in Addison's dream of reaching her grandparents' farm began to fade. "Why? Why would you—"

Emma hung her head. Tears dripped onto the blanket, soaked into the wool. "I have to find—"

Panic overloaded Addy's system. How was she supposed to take care of herself and the girl?

"I'm going home, Emma. To my grandparents' farm. That's it. I'm not taking you back to where we came from. And definitely not back to Virginia. My goal is not to find Sean. I don't know what the hell you were thinking here?"

Emma looked up, eyes glassed over with tears that couldn't find her cheeks. "Take me with you." She spoke as soft as a mouse's whimper. "I can help when we reach the farm. I can hunt, clean, take care of animals."

Addison sat there, her mind racing through scenarios.

Emma continued, "I know my dad will find me as long as I'm here. If I left with Turk and the others, he'd never see me again. At your grandparents', there's a chance. Right? He knew about the farm. You told him."

Addison slowly nodded in response to the girl. Sean did know about the farm. But that wasn't what her mind chewed on at that

30

moment. All the supplies she had, the weeks of food, the backup arsenal, it was all cut in half now. And not only did she have to keep her own ass safe from the hordes of afflicted, which wasn't too difficult if she was cautious, she now had to watch over a twelve-year-old girl.

"I can hold my own," Emma said, now steeled in her resolve. It shone through in the look on her face, and in her voice. "And if something happens, and I make a mistake and you'd have to risk your life to save me, just keep going. You won't be held back by me."

Addy took a deep breath and closed her eyes and let her head tip back. The sun shone on her and heated her skin for real this time. "You're crazy, girl." She looked across the boat at Emma. "But I can't just send you back out into the Atlantic on this raft. So tighten up and stick close to me. Got it?"

Emma nodded and reached for the oar. She plunged it into the water, disrupting the calm surface. Little whirlpools spun out from the side and died five feet away. The small raft cut through the water. Ten strokes later they slid to a stop on a short, sandy beach bordered with tall reeds and grass.

Addy rose and reached behind her back where the Glock 19 was holstered. It was smaller than the Glock 17, and probably a better fit for the girl. Though she figured a .22 or .380 would have been the best match. She knew from talks with Sean, and experience watching Emma, that the girl could handle the weapon. But when crunch time hit, when Emma had a branch on her leg pinning her down and six afflicted bearing down on her, could she pull off enough perfect shots to survive? What if Addy's life depended on the girl? She shook off the thoughts as Emma took the pistol and scooped up the duffel, threading her arm through it and tossing it over her back.

"You sure you got that?"

Emma staggered left, right, then steadied herself. "Sure."

31

"We don't need everything in there." Addy reached out for the bag. Emma leaned over and let it slide to Addy's hand. She went through it again, lightening the load, then handed it back. "Here, this is better. We'll look for a backpack as soon as we find a store."

They set off, first through the muddy marshlands, taking their time and keeping the surroundings in check. A distant song filled the morning. A bird. One of the remaining few, it seemed, still filled with enough inspiration to let the world know it was time to get moving.

Addy kept her pistol in hand but wouldn't allow Emma to travel the same. The girl carried a machete that Turk had packed. Addison had planned on leaving it behind, which she now realized would be a mistake. It was a solid choice in these times, where you might have to slice into the decaying flesh of a monster looking to eat your face as an appetizer. The girl demonstrated competence with the weapon, slicing through the reeds and hacking away when they reached a thicket of bushes.

Now they lingered along a roadway. Addison believed it was the one Turk had pointed out, and if they followed it generally toward the south, they'd come across the road that led to the horse farm. After a mile she was proven correct when she spotted a lingering street sign.

The woods thinned along the side of the road, giving way to a stretch of small, square, brick ranch houses with what were once neat little square yards surrounded by chain-link fencing. They stuck to the right of the road, behind the houses, hidden by the trees. They were almost past the stretch when Emma screamed and collapsed out of Addison's sight.

FIVE

BETH'S FRAIL GASPS ECHOED ACROSS THE OPEN ROOM. RIVERS OF sweat slid across her forehead, cascaded down her cheeks, despite the frigid temperatures in the room. It had been a long night of constant contractions. The pace was near frantic now, and, best Sean could tell, she was fully dilated. A dark tuft of matted hair was visible under the sheet that covered her legs.

Sean and Leo used the couch cushions and blankets Leo brought from the closet to make a bed for Beth. The cushions spread out as she writhed in pain and fought against them with every contraction.

For her part, Beth kept her screams to a minimum. She squeezed their hands. She bit down hard on a thick chunk of blanket wrapped around a stick the diameter of Leo's thumb. And during the minutes in between, her pants settled to breaths, and her eyes closed, and she dozed for a few seconds at a time, only to be awoken again by the pain of her body expelling the child.

Leo stood in front of the kitchen sink. He wiped the fog on the window created by their breath with a square dish towel. Swirling streaks coated the glass, but he could see outside now.

"How much longer?" he asked without looking back.

Sean checked the baby's progress again, though he hadn't needed to. "Could be minutes. Could be an hour."

Leo turned, leaned back against the sink. "Anything we can do?"

Sean pushed off his knees and rose and joined the man. He turned the spigot. Wishful thinking. There was no water running? Everything they had was in various stages of melting in the three steel pots they found in the cabinets. He wiped his hands on his pants and leaned back against the counter next to Leo.

"Ever worked on a farm?" Sean said.

Leo shot him a sideways glance, mouth open a crack as though he'd be awfully comfortable with a cigarette there. "No. Not sure what you mean, either."

"Sometimes you run into a situation with the cattle. A breech."

"Like a sideways baby?"

"Exactly."

"That what's happening here?"

"No, it's not that." Sean lowered his voice even more. He didn't want to upset Beth. If she thought her baby was in danger, she might not be as steeled in her resolve to keep noise to a minimum. "At some point, we gotta worry about the baby though. Too long in the current position could result in a massive decrease in heart rate. And without enough blood pumping around...well, you can guess."

"Jesus."

"There's more, and it could be worse."

"What the hell could be worse?"

"The umbilical cord."

"What about it?"

"Could be wrapped around the baby's neck."

"Well, what are we gonna do, Sean?"

We? Sean thought. All Leo had been good for was fetching more snow for the water buckets and lending his hand for Beth to crush. The man was rubbing his right hand at that moment and flexing his fingers, a grimace across his face.

"Here's what we're gonna do," Sean said. "We're not gonna panic. The contractions are coming at three to three-and-a-half minutes now. This is almost over. Beth's been resting for a while now. I haven't been nagging on her to push. But it's time. She needs to give everything she's got, and for that, you need to do the same."

Leo nodded and said nothing.

"Can you do that? Do you have it in you?"

But before Leo could answer, they heard Marley outside. The bark was ferocious, and non-stop for several seconds. Leo spun away from Sean, toward the window. He wiped frantically with his rag on the glass and put his face to it.

"Can't see a damn thing through all that snow," he said.

Sean reached around his back and grabbed his pistol. "I'll go check this out."

Beth drew a sharp breath, bit her bottom lip hard and moaned. She covered her eyes with the back of her left forearm. Her head shook side to side, then her body convulsed as though she had a hundred thousand volts running through her. Her foot knocked one of the pots over. Fortunately, it was the most recent, and a small avalanche of snow spilled out. She pulled her arm away from her face and began to cry, muttering something about not being able to do this.

Leo grabbed Sean by the shoulders and squared up to him. He looked past Sean, though, toward the window, toward the sound of Marley's incessant barking.

"You stay here with her," Leo said. "I'll go investigate this."

"Let me," Sean said. "It's better that I—"

"No." His gaze shifted to the pistol. "I'm guessing by now you know how to use that thing. So, keep a watch over her should whatever's out there get past me."

Sean tried to argue again, but Leo was at the front door with a knife in one hand, and the towel in the other. What was his plan for the towel? Who knew why anyone did the things they did these days.

A cold blast of air whipped through the room. Leo struggled with the door. The wind wanted to smash it into the wall. He dipped his shoulder into it, opening it wide enough to slip out. Then he dropped the towel and wrapped his hand around the knob and fought against the wind to close it. The room went quiet after an audible hushing sound. Sounded that way, at least.

Sean watched through the fogging window until Leo was lost in the whiteout. He waited there for a few extra moments and realized that Marley's barking had subsided. Was it because Leo was out there? Or had the threat abated?

The final thought that ran through Sean's mind was one he didn't want to face. What if something had happened to the dog?

He turned away from the window and gave his attention back to Beth.

"How're you holding up, hon?" he asked.

"What's going on out there? Where's Leo?"

"He's getting some more ice."

She licked her cracked, dry lips, and a smile spread. He hadn't noticed how perfect her teeth looked until that moment. Like bright white chiclets. How had she managed to keep them so clean looking all these months? Perhaps she packed a year's supply of whitening strips. But would that matter anymore?

"I know that's not true," she said.

"How so?" Sean said.

"Because you wouldn't have stood there at the window watching him."

Sean shrugged and said nothing.

"And he would've taken that pot I knocked over out there with him."

"Guess you got me."

"I heard the dog barking." She lifted her head and looked Sean in the eye. She grimaced and sucked in a quick breath. "What's his name?"

"Marley."

"Seems like a good dog."

"He is. Saved my ass more than once, that's for sure."

"He yours?"

"Belonged to a friend." He tried to keep his gaze focused on her and not let it drift while he thought about Barbara and ultimately, his wife Kathy.

"Well, you're a good friend keeping him around for her."

"How'd you know she's a her?"

Beth shrugged and smiled, though it looked more like an attempt trying to work a hunk of meat free from her teeth. "Just a hunch." She lowered her head back onto the pillow and stared up at the ceiling. "Anyway, what do you say we get this baby out of me?"

Sean glanced back at the door, then the window, which had fogged over again. What he wouldn't give for a bark or a yell or a bang against the door at that moment. Something to let him know Leo was holding his ground out there. He was hesitant to begin the final push without the other man present. What if something happened outside in the middle of it all? He couldn't leave the woman alone in that position. Once it started, there was no turning back.

"Let's wait for Leo," he said, looking back at the door. "I'll feel better when he's back."

"Sure," Beth said. "Because this is all about how you feel, right?"

Sean swung his head around and saw that same pained smile flashing at him. He chuckled softly, mostly to himself, lowered his nodding head. When he glanced up again, she was still staring at him. The grin had faded somewhat.

"Another one's coming," she said.

Sean's first instinct was to ready for an afflicted, but the reality of the present situation set in and he understood her words to mean another contraction. How long was it since the last? He'd lost track, not that it was easy to keep up with the exact timing. But he had a general idea.

He lifted the sheet and saw the top of the baby's head. It might only take one more good round of pushing to get the baby out.

"Ready?" she asked.

He held up a finger. "I need to check."

She rolled her eyes and let her head drop back to the pillow and her feet to the floor. Didn't bother with the sheet, leaving everything below the waist exposed.

Sean went to the window, wiped it with the rag, leaving swirling condensation streaks. The visibility was maybe ten feet past the porch. Not enough. So he grabbed his coat and armed himself with his pistol and opened the front door. A swift wind penetrated. Beth called out something about freezing her lady parts off. Sean ignored her and slipped through the opening, pulling the door shut behind him.

"This is crazy," he muttered to himself. What was he doing? A woman lay inside, a baby ready to exit her body. And here he was, wandering around in a snowstorm trying to get himself killed.

Leo's tracks stood out in the deep powder. Sean followed them away from the porch. They went out straight for thirty feet, then cut to the right. He peered off in that direction looking for any trace of the guy.

Over the howling whistle of the wind through the barren trees, he heard Beth's muffled screams span a solid fifteen seconds before tapering off. She couldn't remain alone much longer.

Sean followed the tracks another fifty yards. He glanced back often, but by this point, the small cabin had retreated from view behind the snowy veil. Not even three minutes had past. But anything could happen in a hundred and eighty seconds.

He butted up to a thick tree and covered his eyes with both hands after tucking the pistol in his coat pocket. It didn't help. He could see no further. Only thing it did was keep a few flakes from hitting his face. He was ready to return. And as he started to do so, he caught sight of a faint outline approaching from the direction of Leo's tracks.

Sean took cover behind the tree, pistol in hand, peeking out a few times until he had a better view of the incoming being. Chances were it was Leo. But it could be an afflicted. If so, he'd have to begin a retreat careful to remain out of sight of the dead.

He eased out again. The person heading toward him stopped. Sean got a good look at the guy who was still blurred by the snowfall. The height and frame appeared right.

"Hey-o," the guy called out while waving his hand.

Sean shook his head, stepped out from the tree. He waited there for Leo to meet him.

"Any sign of Marley?" Sean asked.

The guy swung his head side to side. "Not a damn thing out there right now. Guess whatever it was, your boy's still giving chase." He smiled and gave Sean a pat on the shoulder. "Maybe he'll bring us back a deer."

"That'd be—"

A shrill scream from the direction of the cabin stopped him short.

"That's not Beth." Leo burst past Sean. He kicked up snow as he raced toward the cabin.

"Leo!" Sean said, but it was too late. The man wasn't stopping.

In his mind, he was the last line of defense for the woman and his unborn niece or nephew.

Leo disappeared from sight. Another shrill yell rang out. It was coming from beyond the cabin. Sean took off, sticking to the path Leo had carved out for him.

When he reached the cabin, the other man had an afflicted pinned to the ground, face-first in the snow. Leo was pulling his knife free from the back of the dead's head. He wiped the blade in the snow. Long red tracks stood out. By the time Sean reached them, fresh powder had dulled it to a soft pink.

"Ready to deliver a baby?" Sean asked.

Leo looked up, laughed a soundless laugh, and nodded.

Five minutes later they were on the floor preparing for Beth's final push. Leo knelt at her side, offering his hand as a crushing pad. Sean had his right hand underneath the crown of the baby's head. Held his left over top. He looked like Carlton Fisk waiting for the first pitch in the final game of the World Series.

"All right, Beth," he said. "Let's do this."

The dreaded silence after the baby was born sucked whatever heat there was out of the room. The umbilical cord was wound and knotted around the infant's neck. Sean worked to free it. Seconds were precious. The little one could only last so long without air. It was a boy, and he moved his arms and legs like he was trying to swim to freedom.

Sean unknotted and unwound the umbilical cord from around the infant's neck, then sucked the warm, salty fluid from its mouth and nose. He leaned over to spit it out, still holding the baby over his mother. He hadn't righted himself when the little guy's first choppy cries escaped his little mouth.

Leo was the first to start crying, followed by Beth, who held the baby tight to her chest and kissed the top of his head repeatedly. Sean couldn't help but join in. The moment was powerful, but so were the memories of Emma's birth. And they raced through his mind.

The moment lasted several minutes. The baby's cries faded as he found his mother's breasts and the food supply contained within. Leo curled up next to mother and child. And Sean washed his hands in the pot that was half snow, half water.

Everything was fine. For now.

But now didn't last long.

And everyone's face drained as they looked up at the door after a loud series of knocks.

SIX

TURK AWOKE TO A SLICE OF LIGHT THAT KNIFED ACROSS HIS FACE. HE opened his eyes and blinked Elana's silhouette into focus. She slipped into the room and closed the door behind her after flicking on the light. Turk pulled himself into a sitting position, hunched over his knees. He rubbed his eyes and then stretched.

"Time is it?" he asked.

"Almost eight," she said.

"Shit."

"Well, you didn't come to bed until almost five." She sat on the edge of the bed, right knee drawn up, facing him. She reached for his hand and squeezed. "You okay?"

"Just couldn't stop thinking of how I failed Sean." He wouldn't look at her. Didn't want her to see the misting on his eyes.

Elana leaned forward and dipped her head so he couldn't avoid her stare. "She made a decision, Turk."

"She's a kid. It wasn't her decision to make. I was in charge...I mean, I was responsible for her. If something happens, what am I supposed to say?" He looked up. "If Sean shows up on the island, looking for his little girl, what am I supposed to tell him?"

"That she left. She did it on her own accord. You couldn't stop her because she didn't give you a chance to stop her. Whatever the reason, she decided to get back to shore. Maybe she's got a fantasy that she can find her dad? Frankly, who do you think you are to stop her from doing so?"

"Who am I?" Turk thudded his sternum with the tip of his index finger. "Christ, I'm the guy tasked with taking care of all these folks."

"You're not responsible for saving the world anymore, babe."

"Like hell I'm not."

She nudged his chin toward her with her fingers. "Layla, me, hell, even Sarah and those other girls on this boat. That's who you gotta watch out for now. We're the whole world to you. Got it?"

He inhaled a deep breath of stale air and nodded. Dwelling on what had happened, and what events might transpire, proved a waste of energy. What point was there? He'd face Sean when he faced him. Would living the event a hundred times in his mind help? Hell no. It only served to keep him from preparing for events that would certainly happen. Facing the afflicted again, for one. And the ever-present threat of humans not known to him. No one could be trusted.

No one.

"I'll make you some coffee," Elana said, and she kissed him on the forehead and left the room.

He watched her leave and waited until the door clicked shut before throwing back the sheets covering his legs. The room was warm and still. He threw on a pair of shorts and a t-shirt and exited into the galley.

Paige and his daughter Layla sat at one end of the table with a coloring book and crayons spread out in front of them. They'd lucked out in that the boat was stocked with things to keep children busy.

Sarah and Jenny watched him as he crossed to the counter where his wife stood with his coffee in hand. Elana handed him the mug, then lifted her eyebrows and jutted her chin to the young women.

"What?" Turk asked.

"Looks like they have some questions," she said.

Turk lowered his chin to his chest, inhaled the steam from his drink, and sighed. He could put off having the talk, but that would only make it more difficult. He grabbed a stool and dragged it across the room so he could sit in front of them.

"No point in beating around the bush," he said. "Addy wanted a chance to find her grandparents, and I didn't feel right standing in her way."

Sarah said, "But what about Emma?"

Turk nodded and chewed on his bottom lip for a moment. "She must have overheard Addy's plan—"

"Addy told us all she was going," Sarah said. "Before she told you. Emma was there, heard it all."

"So that's how she knew," he said, more to himself than the women. "And I left the damn raft unwatched long enough for her to get on and hide herself under the blankets."

Turk laced his fingers behind his head. The stubble scratched his palms.

"You can't blame yourself," Jenny said. "She wanted her dad to find her. She was scared she'd never see him again."

Turk thought of Becky, the daughter he knew he'd never see again, and stifled back tears that desperately wanted to escape.

"Are you gonna tell the little ones?" Sarah asked. "'Cause I'll do it. I think I can break it pretty gently to them. They both looked up to Emma, her smarts and toughness."

The first tear slipped past Turk's defenses and down his cheek.

He spun on the stool and hopped off. He turned the dry side of his face toward Sarah and Jennie. "That'd be helpful."

On deck he found Jerry at the wheel staring steadfast over the expansive Atlantic. The man jumped when Turk came up behind him and placed his hand on Jerry's shoulder.

"Christ Almighty," Jerry said.

"C'mon," Turk said. "Former Marine? Shouldn't have scared you."

"Once a Marine, always a Marine. And you did scare me." He looked over his shoulder, past Turk, and the spreading wake behind them. "I've spotted another vessel back there."

Turk followed the man's gaze and stared off at the horizon, but there was no ship there. "When's the last time you saw them?"

"'Bout twenty minutes, I guess. Was easier to see them before the sun came up."

Turk reached across Jerry and slowed the engine down. By his calculations, the fuel Jerry and his family had provided was enough to reach the Bahamas. Once in the calmer waters surrounding the islands, it'd be easier to travel by sail.

It wasn't long before the other boat appeared. Turk looked through a pair of binoculars and didn't care for what he saw.

"What is it?" Jerry asked.

Turk handed him the binoculars. "Take a look for yourself."

Jerry put them up to his face and dialed them into focus. "Those dudes don't look too friendly."

The two men on the bow were armed with assault rifles.

"Pirates?" Jerry asked.

"Hard to say," Turk said. "But I doubt they're part of the welcoming committee." He switched positions with the man and took over the controls. "Get Alec and Rhea, and ready yourselves for a fight."

"You got it." Jerry started for the stairs.

"Jer—wait a sec." Turk waited for the man to return. "Have them come up here first."

Jerry disappeared below deck and returned a minute later with Alec and Rhea. The woman shielded her eyes against the sun peeking out from behind dark, racing clouds.

"Take a look behind us," Turk said before pausing a beat. "I don't think those dudes are cruising back there with good intentions. Pretty sure they see another boat, and their only thought is to loot it and kill the passengers. Jerry, how long ago did you first notice them?"

Jerry shook his head and scrunched up his shoulders, which had a similar effect on his face. "You know, I'd like to say about four hours ago. Like I said, before the sun came up, they were easier to spot. At first, I didn't pay it no mind. But they kept showing up regularly."

Alec the cop said, "Must've wanted to see if we were situationally aware. Maybe they figure a lax target is an easier one."

"Something tells me those guys don't care either way," Turk said. "Anyone think they can hit them a thousand meters out in these conditions?"

Jerry half-raised his hand. "I'd be willing to attempt it."

"I don't know if attempting is our best bet. We fire first, we better feel damn confident we're gonna hit something because they'll come at us full force after that."

Rhea asked, "What's the fuel situation like?"

"At the pace we've been running, we can last past Grand Bahama before needing to switch to sail."

"And if we open it up to get away from these guys?" she asked.

Turk stared past her at the boat in the distance. "Hard to say." Then he looked ahead, in the direction they traveled. "If it gets us out of their range and off their radar, then it's worth it. I can get this boat into calmer waters by sail alone. I'd prefer to be there already, but it's not exactly the worst-case scenario."

"Looks like quite a storm brewing," Rhea said.

"It does," Turk said. "Might work to our benefit."

"You're not thinking...?"

"I am."

She stepped up so they were side by side. "Right into it?"

"Full speed ahead." He looked back, stopping to look into her eyes for a moment. "Chances are those guys can match pace with us. Will they want to if we're heading into a thunderstorm?"

She lifted an eyebrow. "Only one way to find out."

"All right." Turk faced the wheel again and barked out a few orders. "Jerry, round up every life vest you can find on this ship. Alec, I want you and Rhea to ready all the rifles. I want everything fully loaded with a spare magazine. There's a few .22 pistols down there. Get the girls together and go over how to use them."

"The girls?" Alec said. "You sure about that?"

"I don't know how many people there are on that boat behind us. But I do know, if they manage to get past us, it won't be but one or two making it below deck. Let's give them a fighting chance, okay?"

Alec nodded and grabbed Rhea by the elbow and the two of them headed out of sight.

Jerry filled the void next to Turk. "My boys, they're ready to pitch in, too."

"They can shoot?"

"What do you think?"

"I'm gonna say you were one hell of a Marine."

"Still am, squid."

Turk chuckled at the guy, then said, "They're your boys. Putting you in charge of them. You feel good with a rifle in their hands, then I do too."

"All right, man."

"But first get those life jackets ready." He looked out at the thickening clouds to the south. "We might be heading into a monster."

Jerry opened up the storage holds on the deck and retrieved two armfuls of life vests. He dropped them by the stairs and went back. He knelt down again and this time pulled out six snorkels and full-face masks. He stopped by Turk on his way down to show off the find.

"Good deal," Turk said. "I'm sure those'll come in handy. Now tell everyone down there to get ready. I'm opening this bitch up."

Jerry walked off, shoulders back, proud of his work. That was all anyone could ask for these days. Lord knows, sitting around and sulking would only send you down the path of the afflicted.

Turk waited two minutes for everyone to prepare, and then he went full throttle. The engine roared and the bow lifted in response as the boat cut through the rolling waves on a course that headed straight into the storm. Shortly after, he grabbed the binoculars and looked back at the other ship. It was giving chase. The men up front had disappeared, but their intentions were clearer than ever.

SEVEN

"WE KNOW YOU ASSHOLES ARE IN THERE."

The man sung the words and knocked rhythmically on the door at the same time.

Sean sat with his back to the door, facing Leo and Beth. The woman pulled the blanket up and wrapped both arms around her baby. Leo sat up. Vapor trails dissipated in the air with every breath he took. The two of them stared wide-eyed at Sean. If they were quiet enough, would the men go away? Another series of knocks, rapid and loud, answered that question.

"How long were you guys here?" Sean asked in a whisper.

"A week," Leo answered. "Never had anyone come up to the door in that time."

The man outside shouted, "If you don't open up this door, then we're gonna have to break it down, and that won't be a good thing."

A few laughs followed the comment.

Passersby? Sean wondered. A couple of guys hellbent on

screwing with someone? In the middle of a storm, though? Didn't make much sense. But what did these days?

He glanced around the room. There wasn't much in the place he felt he needed to hide. Only Marley's leash. He rarely had it on the dog but leaving it out would alert the men to the dog's presence. Sean grabbed it and stuffed it underneath the sink. He used the opportunity to peek through the window. The fog on it made it impossible to see outside.

They banged on the door again.

"This is your last opportunity. If you don't open up, we're gonna assume you're one of *them*, and you know what will happen after that."

The distinctive *chunk-chunk* of a pump shotgun echoed through the small room.

"Let them in," Leo said.

Sean reached for his pistol as he approached the door.

"No," Leo said, placing his hand over the baby's head. "That's only gonna lead to a fight. It's probably just some backwoods guys, tracked us here, wanna see if they can shake us down. We don't have anything they want. They'll leave, Sean. I know it."

"I can hear you." The guy was back to singing. "Are you gonna make me count to three?"

Sean let go of his security, let go of the pistol, and reached for the door knob.

"One."

He unlocked it and turned the handle and pulled the door open. Cold air knifed through, working its way through every opening in his clothing. It chilled him to the core. The door swung hard at him as one of the men drove his shoulder into it from the outside. Sean stumbled back and almost toppled over when he had to balance on his makeshift prosthetic.

A short squatty guy with a deep receding hairline and bushy eyebrows stepped in first. He had on a red-and-black-checkered flannel and jeans and a pair of black boots. He took in the scene, first eyeing Sean. He chuckled a little when he saw the hunk of wood poking out from beneath Sean's pants. Then the guy looked at the trio on the floor.

"How sweet," he muttered, then he looked over his shoulder. "It's clear, boss."

The next man to enter was the opposite of the first. He was tall, lean, had a full head of hair that stood three inches high and had begun to grow out in the back. It was light brown, as was his beard. He had on black cargo pants and a black ski jacket to match. The silver barrel of a revolver poked out from his right sleeve.

The door slammed shut. The third man remained outside.

"What do we have here?" the tall guy said as he glanced around the room after walking to the other corner. His gaze settled on the baby's head, poking out from underneath the blanket. He wagged a finger between Sean and Leo. "Let me guess: you're not sure who the father is? Am I right?" He grinned, wide and toothy. "I'm right. You know I am. Just admit it."

The guy's smile didn't fade, but the short squatty guy wasn't having any of it. He eyed Sean with a meanness Sean hadn't seen in some time.

"I came across them out there. They were being attacked. Her husband—"

The tall guy held up his free hand to silence Sean. "I really don't give a shit about what happened out there."

Sean found himself nodding while he assessed the situation here. The guy walked in like he owned the place. Stood there with far too much confidence considering he was in the presence of three strangers. Had these men been watching them the entire time? Christ, had they led Marley away? Was that the disturbance?

"My concern," the tall guy said, "is what the hell you people

53

are doing in one of our houses when you haven't paid a dime of rent?"

"We didn't know," Leo said.

The tall guy squinted at Sean as his smile faded. He shifted his gaze over to Leo. "Are you the one I should be talking to here? 'Cause, frankly, you look like a little bitch on the floor there, and I don't want to deal with you."

"You can talk to me," Sean said.

THE SMILE RETURNED as the guy shifted his focus to Sean. "I can talk to you."

"That's right." Sean paused a beat. "She went into labor. We just needed a safe place to deliver the baby."

"Oh shit," the guy said. "You mean you got all that placenta and vaginal juices and shit all over my floor?" He glided across the room and squatted down in front of Beth. "No, it's worse than that. You actually soiled my damn cushions? Jesus, you people are monsters. Complete and total monsters." The smile on his face spread as he rose and turned back toward Sean.

"We had no choice. Would've been suicide to remain out there."

The guy hummed a tune Sean recognized as the theme song to M*A*S*H. He wasn't sure what to make of the man and his high level of confidence. Anyone who made it this far into the ordeal with the afflicted had to have some sense about them. Why was this guy sure he was so superior over the small group?

A stifled cry from the baby broke the silence. The tall guy glanced around as though he were about to address a crowd of hundreds.

"Oh wow, that is gonna be a problem," he said. "The hell were you thinking getting knocked up during this shitstorm against humanity?"

Beth tightened her grip on the infant and said nothing.

The tall guy crossed the room toward her. When Sean shuffled forward, the guy stopped and held out his hand without ever looking in his direction. The man's smile returned, though, as he continued toward Beth and Leo. He stopped a few feet short.

"Come on, lemme see the little guy, or gal, whatever the case may be."

Tears spilled past Beth's eyelids and snaked down dried tracks on her cheeks. She pulled the blanket over the child's head.

The tall guy ran his hand through his hair and muttered to himself, "The hell is wrong with these people." His voice rose. "Do they not know who I am?" Then he shouted. "Do you not know who I am?"

Beth looked up at the guy, who now wore a snarl in place of that shit-eating grin. "Wh-what do you want?"

"What I want is for you good folks to recognize the man in front of you."

"Get to the goddamn point," Sean said. "Quit it with the show you're putting on."

The guy turned toward Sean. The antagonized look faded, giving way to that smile once again. He took a few steps forward but stopped well out of Sean's reach.

"You're, like, the leader here, right?"

Sean hung his head and shook it. "I'm no leader."

"Well, you're probably right about that. But every group has to have someone in charge, and I'm betting you're that guy."

"I only met them today. They needed help. I offered it."

"He's right," Beth said. "My dead husband and brother-in-law here, they were trying to get me to a camp where I could have the baby. This man, he helped us. Delivered my baby."

"Camp?" The guy turned so he could see everyone. "We've come from a camp. Were you coming to see us?"

"I doubt that," Leo said.

"Why's that?"

"The people we were going to see wouldn't treat a lady who just birthed a child like this."

The guy put his hands on his knees and leaned forward. "Well, how would they treat an asshole?"

Leo's face tightened, lips bunched, nostrils flared.

The guy straightened up again, put his hands on his hips, and twisted in each direction. "Maybe like this?" He drove his boot into Leo's side. Leo had no chance to deflect the blow. It caught him under the ribs and bowled him over.

Sean started to move. The short squatty guy who'd remained silent the entire time pushed off the wall and intercepted him.

"Get your hands off me," Sean said.

The guy didn't budge. He pushed Sean backward.

"I said get your hands off me."

"Percy," the tall guy said. "Ease off him." He came back into view as Percy stepped to the side. His eyes were wide with wonder and seemed to dance as they flicked side to side while staring at Sean. "Who exactly are you, friend?"

"Ain't your friend," Sean said.

"Yeah," the tall guy said. "You're not. We don't even know each other's names."

Sean stood tall, said nothing.

"Ok, I guess I'll go first. Medrick's the name, and you can call me Medrick."

Sean still said nothing.

Medrick narrowed his eyes as he studied Sean. "Are you saying we can't be friends, friend?"

Percy, who'd been kneeling next to Leo, rose and tugged on Medrick's sleeve. "You might want to check this out, boss."

Medrick wagged his finger at Sean as his smile returned. He held his gaze for a few moments, then turned to his subordinate. "What is it this time?"

"Our guy here, looks like he's been bit by one o' them."

The playfulness was erased from Medrick's face, and this time it was not replaced with a look of anger, but rather concern. Any *society* present these days did not want to bring an afflicted in. He pulled back his sleeve, exposing the revolver completely.

"What happened here?" he asked.

"It's not from one of the dead," Leo said.

"You sure about that?"

"Yes, dammit, I was fighting them off. Got caught on a broken branch or something."

Medrick flinched. "Or something? That's how you're gonna sell this to me?" He pulled back the hammer and extended the pistol toward Leo's head.

"It's not a bite," Sean said. "I've checked it out. It's a gash."

Medrick lowered the pistol and looked over at Sean. "First, how are you qualified to tell? And B, who says one of them didn't gouge him with their decrepit but unnaturally long cocaine-testing fingernails?"

"Just look at it," Sean said. "You'll see what I mean."

Medrick glanced over at the wound, then at Percy. He muttered, "What do you think?"

Percy shrugged as he yanked at the sleeve surrounding the wound. The fabric tore almost the entirety of Leo's arm. He leaned in and looked at the gash. "Don't look like a bite, but, what if the damned thing was *chewing* on him?"

"Yeah, friend," Medrick said, turning back to Sean. "What if the damned thing was chewing on him?"

"Kill me if you have to," Leo said, drawing all attention toward himself. "But at least let me see that my sister-in-law and nephew reach a safe place."

Percy rose and stepped in close to Medrick, who looked as bemused over the situation as ever. Sean thought the guy didn't care whether Leo lived and travelled or died right there on that floor.

Sean leaned forward and angled his head to hear Percy's words.

"That baby's gonna give us away out there. We can't have that."

"Don't you dare," Sean said.

"Dare what?" Medrick said, playing coy. But Percy had already moved, stripping back the sheets and trying to rip the infant away from its mother.

The scream that came from Beth's mouth could have risen the dead twice. She held on to the baby with one arm and flailed her other, catching Percy square on the nose. As he stumbled backward, she began kicking. Several of the blows landed in his gut and crotch. He fell back against the wall, clutching both areas.

Leo was on his feet, about to take on the man.

Medrick had backed up to the wall where he yelled something out. He aimed the pistol at Leo.

The door crashed open, and the third man entered. He was a medium build Hispanic guy with short dark hair littered with specks of silver. He swung the pump shotgun around the room while joining in with the shouting.

Finally, thunder erupted when Medrick fired his pistol.

EIGHT

ADDISON SCRAMBLED THROUGH THE THICK UNDERBRUSH TOWARD the place where she'd last seen Emma standing. The girl called out for help, her voice sounding tiny and pained. As Addy ascended the small hill Emma had been traversing, it became apparent what had happened. The girl had fallen into a hole that someone had covered.

"Addy!" Emma yelled.

The faster Addison moved, the more the terrain tried to restrain her. She had to stop and free herself from vines that snaked across the landscape, hidden by a thick layer of dead and decomposing foliage.

"Please, come quick," Emma called out, her voice floating out of the four-foot-wide hole.

"Quiet," Addy said as loudly as she dared. She dropped to her knees as the trap drew near. There could be others dug out nearby, or the ground next to it could be weak and ready to collapse. They'd be good as dead if both of them ended up in there. She worked her fingertips into the soil beneath the leaves and vines and pulled herself forward foot by foot. When she was near the edge, she planted her knees in the ground and stretched forward as though she were performing an awkward yoga pose with her head and neck craned as far as they'd go.

"Help." Emma looked up at her, tears in her eyes. The girl was sitting with her right leg drawn up to her stomach, hands wrapped around her ankle.

"You okay?"

Emma shook her head. "Foot hurts."

"Can you stand?"

Emma scratched at the wall of packed dirt and grabbed hold of the uneven surface and pulled herself to her feet. "Think so."

Addison dropped to her stomach and reached her hand down. But it was no use. At least three feet of air stood between their outstretched digits. She pulled away from the opening.

"Where are you going?" Emma's voice was a few decibels too loud.

Addy turned back, looked down at the girl, and placed her finger over her lips to tell Emma to be quiet. Then she moved away again. She sat there for a few moments, taking in their surroundings. Was anyone out there? Watching and waiting for the right moment to move in? What about the afflicted? Had they heard the commotion?

As she rose, Addy made the pistol a little more accessible and retrieved her knife. It wasn't solely for protection, though. She had an idea. Throughout their travels they'd come across these thick wild grape vines. Some were four inches or so in diameter. If she could find one and cut a chunk off, she could pull Emma out of the hole with it.

She walked to the edge of the pit, a little less concerned about it caving in. "I'm going to find something to get you out of there."

Emma nodded and said nothing.

"You got that little Glock on you?"

60

Emma's eyes widened as she seemed to recall the pistol at that moment. She reached behind her back.

"Don't take it out now," Addison said. "Just be ready if you hear some commotion out here. Okay? Don't be stupid about it."

Emma gave her a thumbs-up. Addy winked back at her. The girl caught on quick. Too bad she hadn't been a little more cautious approaching the trap. But Addy knew she couldn't lay all that blame at the girl's feet. After all, she was twelve and stuck in this shitty situation without her father. She'd gone from expecting him to be around to take care of her, to out on her own. But wasn't that due to her own actions? She could have remained safe with Turk.

A selfish thought raced through Addison's mind, sending a shock through her system as she tried to squash it before it materialized. What if she left the girl? No one but her knew they'd been together.

"Don't even go there," she muttered to herself.

The turmoil inside following that thought lasted a full two minutes. Probably would've gone on longer, but she performed a mind dump the moment what she had been searching for appeared.

The vine hung a good five feet off the ground. She grabbed the end and tugged. Her hope had been that it would give a good amount and she'd cut what she needed. But the vine didn't budge.

Addy tucked the knife in the sheath and wrapped her arms and legs around the tree and worked her way up six inches or so at a time. She reached the first branch, which stretched out about ten feet off the ground. She threaded one leg around it, then hooked her feet together at the ankles so she straddled the branch.

The vine hung three feet away. She worked down the branch until she had it in hand. The knife had a serrated saw blade on the backside. She worked that through the vine until it was cut about halfway, then began hacking at it with the sharp blade. She alternated like this until she had severed eight feet worth of vine free.

Addy didn't bother scaling down the trunk again. Instead she hugged the branch, let her legs and torso fall, then stretched the length of her body. The fall from that point was hardly noticeable. She hit the ground soft and with bent knees scooped up the vine and started back toward Emma.

No sooner had she begun her trek than the girl screamed. The sound echoed through the woods and was met with replies from the afflicted. Their horrid screeches soon overtook the gentle silence that had been present.

Addison disregarded her safety and sprinted, dodging dead trees, hurdling small bushes, and tripping but not falling on the snaking vines.

She slowed her pace as she approached. Since that scream, she hadn't heard a peep out of Emma. Had something happened?

PLEASE GOD, don't let anything have happened to the girl.

She was sure she couldn't live with it if Emma succumbed to the dead on her watch.

Addy threaded through the final stretch, using the trees as shields. She had the Glock in one hand, the vine looped around the other. Who cared if a gunshot drew attention in this situation? She needed to free Emma as fast as possible and they could take off.

When the small hill came into view, she spotted a single afflicted standing between her and the hole. It was staring up at the trees. Confused, perhaps, about what had made the sound. Those primal instincts brought it to the place it had occurred, but it couldn't find the source.

Addy dropped the vine and retrieved the knife once again. She stepped into the opening, her feet landing softly on the ground.

She tried not to crunch the dead leaves. She circled behind the afflicted, which had once been a short man wearing a suit. Maybe the suit had been blue with pinstripes. Now it was covered in mud and dried blood.

She stood five feet behind the dead. The stench was miserable. If she ever wound up in a room full of shit from ten public toilets, this was what she imagined it would smell like.

Addy drew the knife up, blade aimed at the afflicted.

But before she could plunge it, the dead turned and faced her. Dull eyes flashed to life with yellow and green. It opened its mouth wide. Thick strands of mucus connected top and lower teeth. Bugs feasted on what had once been a tongue. The afflicted started toward her.

She swung with the knife. The blade sunk into its soft cheek and sliced through one side to the other. The afflicted's jaw dropped almost to its chest. She must've severed some remaining connective tissue.

It wasn't enough, though. It reached out and grabbed her shirt. The fabric bunched in its hand. It started to pull her closer.

She stabbed with the knife again. It penetrated through the afflicted's forehead. The lights went out. It released her shirt and collapsed to the ground at Addy's feet.

Addison stumbled backward and dropped the knife as she reached down to steady herself. There could be more traps, she reminded herself. Flailing around out here could lead to a slow and painful death.

Throughout the woods, other afflicted called out. To one another? She could only hope not.

"Addy?" Emma said. "Did you get it?"

She raced back to the tree, scooped up the vine and hurried back to the girl, tossing the stretch of makeshift rope down to Emma. The girl wasted no time. She yanked hard on the vine and grunted.

"You making it?" Addy said. She was a few feet back. Any closer, she might slip down. Emma was small, but the force of her body pulling down was enough that Addison had to brace herself.

"Almost there."

A hand appeared, all bunched into a fist. Then the other. The top of her head and that mane of brown hair followed, with her cute face not far behind.

Addison felt a surge of energy and strength and she pulled hard on the rope while backing up. A moment later, Emma was free. The girl sprinted to Addy. She collapsed in her arms and cried softly.

"You okay?" Addy asked.

"My ankle burns." Emma pushed back and lifted her foot.

Addison looked her over. "Where's your bag?"

The girl closed her eyes and dropped her head back. "Oh, no. I left it in the hole."

"Okay, this isn't as big a deal. We've got the vine now. I can lower you back in, you get it, and I'll pull you back out."

Emma wiped tears away, leaving dirty streaks on the side of her face. "I can do this."

They stood and both faced the hole. Addison's stomach rose into her throat.

Two afflicted were stumbling toward them. But they would never make it all the way. The hole swallowed them alive.

"It-it's okay," Emma said. "We'll shoot them, then I'll go in."

"These woods are crawling with afflicted, Emma. Listen. Do you hear that?"

The calls were incessant between the dead at that moment. The energy of what had occurred raced through the forest, and all of them knew something was going on.

"What's that?" Emma said.

"It's them," Addy said. "The afflicted."

"No, there's something else." She pointed toward the right, back toward the road. "Is that a...horse?"

Addison closed her eyes and faced in that direction. And she heard it, too.

"Come on."

Addy threaded her arm around Emma and helped her down the small hill and through the woods. Though it felt as though they were moving through molasses, it benefitted them. The ground was treacherous. Moving too fast increased the chances of mistakes. Mistakes in this environment led to death.

The horse led them to it with its constant whines. They found the animal tied to a tree trunk, a generous length of rope allowing it freedom to move twenty feet in any direction. At its feet was an afflicted lying still in a puddle of dark blood. There were two others nearby. They stood still, watching, seemingly unsure how to approach the beast.

Addy held Emma back. They remained out of sight. She was fascinated by the scene. Since when did those dead bastards *think*? She swept the surrounding area with her gaze, spotted a rock the size of a softball. Perhaps it could serve as a distraction.

"Wait here," she whispered to Emma, squeezing the girl's shoulders. She dashed across an opening and scooped up the rock. No stranger to heaving a ball, she cocked her arm back and let the rock sail, past the horse, over the heads of the afflicted. It clattered through branches and knocked off the side of a tree trunk.

She held her breath in anticipation.

The afflicted did not move.

The horse was startled, flinched, looked away from the dead waiting to eat it.

And then the afflicted reacted. Not to the horse, but the sound behind them. At almost the same moment, both turned their rotten heads toward the sound. Their bodies followed. They shuffled at different speeds away from the horse.

Addy hurried back to Emma. She found the girl crouching, peering out from the side of her cover.

"Think you can untie it?" Addison asked her.

"I can," Emma answered.

"Approach her from the front, hold out your hand. Once she accepts you, get her untied."

"What are you gonna do?"

"Take care of those two." She straightened and armed herself with a knife from her boot and the Glock 19. "So don't be surprised if you hear gunshots."

Addy led the way into the clearing. The horse glanced over at her for a moment before returning its focus to the afflicted. What had the animal seen over the months since the outbreak? She glanced back and saw Emma approaching as she had instructed. *That's my girl*, she thought. *Nice and easy.*

When Addy stepped on a branch and snapped it in half, one of the afflicted reacted immediately. It froze in place while the other continued on. Addison's heart rose in her throat. She lifted the 9mm. Cold sweat affected her grip on the pistol. She squeezed the grip even tighter. The last thing she wanted to do was fire a shot and draw more afflicted out of the woods.

Several seconds passed. Emma whispered to the horse. Sounded like rustling leaves in the wind. The dead remained still, its head cocked slightly, maybe staring up at the trees. Addy couldn't tell. Couldn't see the damned's face. She lifted the knife eye-height, blade out, and stepped quickly toward it. A single plunge in the back of its head was all it took. The blade cut through the decaying skull like it was mud. Dark blood and mucus-like brain seeped out of the spreading hole as the afflicted slid down and Addy held the knife steady.

She stepped back, away from the mess. The other afflicted had continued to shuffle into the woods, almost out of sight now.

"How are we doing over there?" she said softly.

"Almost got her free," Emma replied, perhaps a little too loudly.

Addison stepped around the clearing, remaining in the skeletal shadows of the tree. They were in the clear, it seemed. She tucked the pistol behind her back and the knife in the oversized sheath, then moved to help Emma.

Since leaving Virginia, she thought the most spine-chilling sound she'd ever hear was those things screeching and howling throughout the night. Laying there, unsure if she'd wake up alive again. Fearing what eternal waking-death would be like.

But at that moment, with Emma at her side and a calm horse next to them watching their every move, the sounds of the afflicted crying out had nothing on the distinct *chunk-chunk* of a shotgun.

"Thanks for taking care of those dead bastards," a guy said. "Now raise your hands and back the fuck away from my horse."

NINE

SEAN TRIED NOT TO FLINCH. HE DIDN'T WANT TO SHOW WEAKNESS IN front of the men. But the deafening sound of the .357 erupting throughout the small cabin was too much. He covered his ears and his head with his forearms and hands and bowed forward a little. It was disorienting, if only for a moment or two.

As the echoes dissipated, another sound took over.

Medrick's laughter.

The guy smoothed back his puffy brown hair and waved the pistol around like it was a toy. The hole in the wall just past Leo and Beth proved it was the real deal, though.

"If you could only see your faces," Medrick said in between bellows. "Holy shit! That was some good stuff."

"You asshole!" Beth pulled her baby tight to her chest in an attempt to muffle its cries. It was only natural for the infant to be upset, but these men might use it as an excuse to kill the kid.

"Percy," Medrick said as he gestured toward the woman.

Percy bent over and grabbed for the infant. Beth turned away from him, cradling the child with one hand, lashing out with the other. Her fingernails caught Percy on the face, left two lines down his left cheek.

"Goddamn you, lady." He smacked her on the back of the head.

The assault drew Leo's ire. He shifted to his knees and dove into Percy, knocking him away from Beth and into the cabin wall. Leo managed a few blows to Percy's ribs before the third guy pulled him off.

"Do I need to use my gun again?" Medrick yelled. "You people are hell-bent on killing yourselves in here." He aimed the weapon at Beth's head. "Look over here, man."

Leo refused to do so. Medrick nodded at the third guy, who grabbed a handful of Leo's hair and forced him to face his sister-in-law.

"You want to see what her brains look like?" Medrick said. "What about the baby's? Ever wonder what a newborn's insides smell like? Because I'm sure as shit happy to show you if you want to keep acting up."

Leo's hardened look softened and tears welled in his eyes.

"That's what I thought," Medrick said, shifting his aim toward Leo. "Now tell me you're sorry."

Leo looked away and said nothing.

Medrick pulled back the hammer. "Tell me you're sorry." He said the words slowly and deliberately, almost like he was counting down a warning.

Sean studied the man. There was an arrogance there. Not that he'd lived any kind of life before the outbreak, not an honorable one, at least. But he had the kind of streak through him that allowed him to capitalize on it. Maybe he'd been that way his entire life, preying on the weak. But there were few weak left. They succumbed to the afflicted. So Medrick stepped up his game. To put fear in those who had strength, he had to appear more terrifying than humanity's common enemy.

Leo held up a hand, shielding his face. "I'm sorry." The words hung in the air between them. For a moment, it appeared Medrick was going to follow through on the threat laid down when he readied his revolver.

The corners of Medrick's lips twitched, giving way to a toothy grin. He de-cocked the .357 and lowered the barrel toward the ground. "That's all I wanted to hear." He nodded at the third guy, who helped Percy off the ground.

Leo turned his back on Medrick and went to Beth's side to check on her and the baby.

Medrick turned to Sean. "Shit is just getting way out of control in here. Wouldn't you agree?"

Sean held the man's steady gaze and said nothing.

"Wouldn't you agree, man?" He paused a beat. "What's your name again?"

"Sean."

Medrick wiped his lips and nose with his sleeve, made a face when he looked at the results. "You delivered that baby?"

Sean nodded.

"You don't look like a doctor. I mean, no offense, but haven't seen many MDs running around, or I guess I should say hobbling around on a wooden leg."

Sean didn't return the guy's smile.

"Anyhoo," Medrick said. "Nurse? Paramedic?"

"Something like that."

Medrick nodded a couple times. "We could use a guy like you. So many people get fucked up daily in this crazy ass world we're living in. Maybe our doc has something better than a twig to stick under your knee. Whaddya think about that?"

Sean didn't respond.

"How'd that happen anyway?" Medrick asked. Then he threw up a finger and put it up to his lips for a moment. "Wait, don't tell me. Military. Right? Got that shit blown off, didn't you?"

"That's right."

Medrick crossed his arms. The barrel of his revolver poked out from under his left armpit. If there were ever a time for Sean to attack, this was it. He glanced at the floor to gauge whether he could clear the distance in one step. Perhaps Medrick read his mind, because the guy dropped his arms and walked away, saying, "We can definitely use a guy like you, Sean."

Was it a foregone conclusion that he'd go? What if he refused?

The baby let out a stifled cry that turned into a yawn. The three men who'd invaded the house all stared down at it. Percy stuck out his index finger with his thumb drawn back. He pretended to fire at the little guy.

"I'll go," Sean said. "I'll go if you'll guarantee safe passage for the infant, and Beth and Leo."

"And if we don't?" Medrick challenged him. "If that little runt starts bawling in the woods and I take it upon myself to silence him?"

Sean shuffled forward, playing up the fact he only had one leg that extended below the knee. "Then you'll get a quick lesson on who I really am."

Medrick's eyes narrowed and he leaned his head to the side as though he wasn't used to anyone speaking to him the way Sean just had, and he was debating on how to handle it. The room went so silent you could hear the draft punching through the shut door.

"Got yourself a deal, Sean." Medrick stuck out his hand, but Sean refused to take it.

"Boss," Percy said. "What about this dude? I still don't like the looks of that gash. What if he turns?"

"Doctor Sean," Medrick said, making a production out of it. "What's your professional opinion of Leo's arm here?"

"Told you already," Sean said. "A gash from a branch, something like that. Needs attention, more than can be provided here. If he turns, it'll be because he dies from infection, not because he's afflicted."

"Hear that, Percy? Doctor Sean has spoken."

"I think he's full of shit," Percy said.

"We'll let Doc decide that. And if he agrees, we'll let these two settle it in the pit." Medrick smiled again as his gaze flitted between Sean and Leo. "Besides, ain't like he's gonna turn on the ride back. You've seen that shit happen. He's gotta die first. We know how to handle that."

Sean focused on the words *ride back*. Did they have a vehicle that could fit them all? If so, was all this about the baby making noise for show? Were they wanting to see how much the small group would resist? Would they have gone as far as to kill the infant?

"You're making a mistake," Percy said.

Medrick's entire demeanor changed. Was it the challenge his subordinate was posing? Was it that he was doing it in public?

"Go get the truck," he said to the third man. Then he walked up to Percy, who retreated to the wall. Medrick spoke low, but not so quiet as to keep Sean from hearing. "Don't know what you think you're doing here, but if you got a problem with how I lead, there's the fucking door. Let's see how long your crying ass can survive out there alone."

Percy jerked his head up and down an inch. His stare never left Medrick's eyes. What was the story there? What kind of history existed between these men? Sean had to find a way to get inside Percy's head and figure a few things out.

"How far?" Sean said.

Medrick turned to look at him. "What?"

"How far to your place?"

"Down the road."

"How long've you been there?"

"A while."

"How many people you got there?"

"Enough to start a war."

"What about—"

Medrick pointed at him. "Let's cut the twenty questions, okay, Sean. I'm doing you a favor here. The least you can do for me is shut up. Got it?"

Sean felt Beth and Leo staring at him. Either they were waiting to see what he would do next or begging for him to glance in their direction so he could see the chastising looks on their faces.

"I'm getting mighty tired of you ignoring me when I ask you a question, Sean." He tugged on the waistband of his pants as he closed the gap between the two of them. "Answer me!"

With the .357 pointing up at his chin, Sean said, "Yeah, I got it." There wasn't much choice in the matter. They weren't walking out of the cabin on their own. If he attempted to overpower Medrick and failed, it wouldn't be only him that would pay. There were others to consider. And though he did not know them, he had committed to them. They were now in his stead, and he had to act for the betterment of the group.

The door swung open and with it came that familiar icy air. The third man stepped back in, and behind him were two more men, armed with assault rifles.

Sean glanced at Medrick, who met his stare with that same toothy smile. The picture grew clearer in his mind. There was no way out. Even if they had killed the three intruders, Sean and Beth and Leo and even the baby would have been shot the moment they exited the house alone.

Medrick leaned in close to Sean and spoke so only Sean could hear him. "You get it now, don't you?"

Sean nodded and said nothing. He watched them escort Beth and Leo through the door. He followed a moment later. The snow fell in sheets now. They trudged a hundred yards or so where a black Ford Excursion waited. They were directed inside the vehicle. An unnamed man with a heavy brown beard kept a black rifle pointed at them in the back seat.

Sean glanced out the side windows and threw a look over his shoulder in search of Marley. If the dog was close, he'd remained hidden. Maybe he'd find a way to keep up. Probably not, though. He began to resign himself that he might never see Marley again.

Medrick climbed in last and eased into the front passenger seat. He pulled down the visor and caught Sean's attention in the vanity mirror.

"I hope you guys are ready to head to your new home."

TEN

THE SKIES WERE BLACK AS NIGHT. THE AREA BETWEEN SEA AND cloud glowed an off shade of green. The waves rolled, some as high as thirty feet, tossing the sailboat about. It was past one in the afternoon. Turk had held on for more than four hours, fighting the storm, doing everything in his power to head into the waves and not be overtaken by them.

The other boat had stayed in heavy pursuit for an hour. Even with Turk's vessel running full throttle, the other ship gained on them. He'd come close to starting to fire warning shots at them. Let them know he wouldn't be taken over easily. Hell, if they knew who he was, and the things he'd done in his career, they would've backed off.

And then Turk wouldn't have led the people he was entrusted to take care of into the middle of a hurricane. Alec had insisted it was a nor'easter, but it was only November. Still hurricane season. They could have debated it all afternoon, had it not been for the nasty conditions. If only the Weather Channel still existed to set them straight on the matter.

When the first wave over twenty feet swept over the deck, the other boat called off its chase. Maybe Turk should've stopped there. Perhaps he should have attempted to skirt the storm, heading inland.

They would've watched for that. And it wasn't only Turk who thought so. Alec, Jerry, and Rhea agreed. And as of right now, they were his inner circle when it came to decisions.

So he pushed forward. And now regretted it.

He was tied off with a thirty-foot length of rope. Gave him enough slack to move about the deck should he need to. Also left plenty for him to be washed overboard. To combat that, he hooked on to the console with a shorter strap. Of course, that posed as many problems as being swept over. If the boat rolled, and he was knocked unconscious, there was no chance of survival.

Below deck, everyone had on life vests. The snorkel gear had been distributed. In the current conditions it'd be useless. But the storm wouldn't last forever.

They'd gone through the eye wall, which meant they'd encountered the toughest part of the storm, northeast of the wall. From here it'd diminish. If only it were that easy.

Exiting out of the calm had been worse than going in. The pattern of the sea had changed. If Turk hadn't adapted as quickly as he did, they would've rolled and every last one of them might've drowned.

Alec came up to check on him every ten to fifteen minutes. He tied off to the stairs leading down. He kept Turk informed on everyone's condition down below. There were a few injuries attributed to the storm, but nothing major.

Now Turk stood alone. The rain pelted him from all directions, soaking him to his core. He welcomed a good rain these days. It cleansed him. Washed away the evil that surrounded the world. But this was too much. If he managed to lead the group out of the storm, he'd probably die of pneumonia. Temperatures on deck were in the fifties, at best. With the heavy winds, he was reminded of cold water training during BUD/s.

It didn't take long to settle back into the rhythmic movement of the sea. Even in chaos, harmony existed. Nature was constantly trying to provide patterns. And this was no different. He continued to pilot the craft, picking the path possible at the given moment. A few times the best he could find led to close calls. The boat had been vertical pointing up, down, and ridden the port and star-board rails a couple of times.

But it stayed afloat.

The ship crested a tall wave. The crash down was going to hurt, Turk could tell. Out of the corner of his eye, he saw some-thing else. Another wave coming at him. He hadn't expected it, and there was no way to avoid it.

Turk hunkered forward, gripped the wheel tight, and readied himself for submersion.

As lightning scratched across the sky through the dark swirling clouds, thunder crashed on the deck. Snapping, tearing, destroying. The mast snapped and hung like a severed spine, resting on the rail.

"Alec!" Turk yelled out. The wind took his words and whisked them toward the sea. He yelled out again.

The sail had been pointless in the storm. He focused on navi-gating, using minimal power from the engines. He'd used a lot of their available fuel getting away from the pirates.

The broken mast posed a different kind of threat. It might swing wildly and hit him or someone else. Or worse, it could somehow penetrate the hull and sink the boat.

He needed Alec, and he needed him on deck now. But he couldn't risk leaving the controls to get the man. Turk shouted again, but his calls were lost to the wind.

The mast swung and slammed into the side of the platform Turk was standing on, and then whipped back the other direction. It wouldn't be long before it did serious damage to the vessel.

The decision ate at Turk. He could hold off the churning sea remaining where he stood, but it might not make a difference if the mast hit him and broke his neck. He rigged the wheel to remain in place. That would keep the ship heading into the waves at an angle so long as there weren't any errant winds. He unclipped himself from the helm and hurried across the slippery deck to the stairs leading below.

"Alec," he yelled out. "I need you up here."

Turk didn't stand idly by after that. He crossed to the broken mast and went to work securing it. If he could get it to remain steady, they had a chance.

The boat turned sharply to the right. Turk took his eyes off what he was doing and noticed the waves coming at him from the side. He cinched off the strap he was working with and dashed across the slippery deck toward the controls.

The boat rose twenty feet, riding the crest on a thin edge. He grabbed onto the rail. They'd either slide back down to the valley or roll and succumb to the force of the ocean. He was strapped in, but getting caught in those churning waters without someone to reel him back meant a certain death.

They descended into the next trough, only to start lifting a few seconds later. Turk hurried to the controls and found his makeshift autopilot cracked. He grabbed the wheel, and as they reached the crest once again, he managed to angle the rudder so they didn't go down entirely sideways. The next wave lifted them, though not as high. Turk fought to right the ship. Before they reached the next trough, they were lifted again, this time head-on.

"Turk!"

He looked over and saw Alec poking his head out of the opening, looking between Turk and the broken mast. The guy didn't linger there, or head up to ask for direction. He crossed the deck and went to work completing the job Turk had started.

A tall wave crashed over the boat from the side. The vessel didn't roll, but a torrent of water slammed into Alec. Turk watched as the water slid off the side and the foam died down.

Alec was gone.

The strap he was attached to was drawn taut.

Without a second thought, Turk left the wheel again. He grabbed onto the strap and walked it to the side. There, he planted his feet against the rail and began yanking. It was tougher than bringing up a marlin. The boat angled sharp left, then right.

"What's happening?" The shout almost slipped away in the wind.

Turk turned and saw Jerry standing there, hands planted firmly on the handrails.

"Alec went overboard," Turk yelled. "Get to the wheel. You can tie off up there."

Jerry nodded and climbed the treacherous staircase to the controls. Turk had no idea if the man knew what he was doing. He couldn't worry about that.

Hand over hand, he pulled on the strap until his muscles begged for him to quit. And then he pulled harder.

Alec emerged from the insidious grip of the sea, his mouth wide open, locked in a silent scream. His hands waved until they landed on the yellow canvas strap. The only thing that kept him alive.

Seeing the man gave Turk a second wind. He pulled harder and faster, and before he knew it, Alec was up against the boat.

Jerry was keeping them steady as he could. They pitched up and down, high and low, but kept cutting through the oncoming waves instead of rolling sideways.

Turk wrapped Alec's strap on a tie-out and leaned over, right arm extended. He bent forward and went as far as he could while leaving one foot on the ground.

Alec's frigid fingers grazed his.

More!

Turk fell back. He took his strap and tied it off too, leaving a little slack. Then he leaned over the rail again, this time letting momentum carry him forward. His feet left the deck. The extra foot was all it took. His hand met Alec's and formed an unbreakable bond. With every last ounce of strength he had left, Turk pulled the man from the mouth of the ocean. Alec swung his free hand and latched onto the railing. Somehow the guy managed to get his head even with the top. His eyes widened as he looked past Turk.

"Watch out," he said.

Turk glanced to the side in time to see the mast had broken free and swung right toward his head. In that split second, he thought about ducking, but the command never reached the correct muscles.

The last thing that went through his mind was how salty the foam tasted as it washed over his face.

ELEVEN

ADDISON FROZE WITH HER HAND ON THE HORSE'S HEAD, SMOOTHING back a tuft of wild brown mane. The deep and slow low-country drawl of the man made him sound relaxed, certainly more so than he could be at that moment. She might be wrong, though, and that thought created a knot so tight in her stomach she thought she might throw up on the poor animal's face.

"Hands up, sweet thing," the guy said. "Don't want to have to kill you or your girl."

Could he see the outline of the Glock under her shirt? She lifted her hand off the horse's head first. As she raised the other, she shifted her hips so that her right side slid out of view.

"That's right," he said. "Just like that. Now take three big steps back. Yeah, one, two, three," he counted as she complied. "Down to your knees."

Addison refused the last command. No chance would she place herself in such a vulnerable position. He'd moved around while speaking, and she had no idea where he stood now. He could be hidden for all she knew.

"Addy," Emma whispered. "Just get down." The girl had already taken her cue and did as the man instructed. Now she looked up at Addison with large, wet eyes.

The entire day had been one step forward followed by multiple small steps back. Small? Hardly. These setbacks had the potential to be huge. She'd never reach her grandparents' farm at this rate.

"Listen, I know you're probably out here trying to survive like most everyone else who's still standing. But you came upon my property, and I'm not taking kindly to that." His shoes thudded against the hard ground as he approached from behind. "This can go one of two ways, and it's entirely up to you. I don't want to hurt you, but I will."

Addison stared at Emma's pale face and the tears that streaked down her cheeks. She had to survive this situation. Who cared if her pride took a blow? She couldn't leave Emma alone with the guy.

"All right," she said. "Don't come any closer."

She turned slowly to face the guy, leading with her left leg.

"What're you doing?"

As she brought her face around, her gaze found a rifle muzzle four feet away. She followed the black barrel to a pair of bright blue eyes that were brought out by a dark brown beard. His forehead was smooth. So was the area around his eyes. He couldn't be much older than her.

He seemed taken aback by Addy, too. "You two sisters?"

"Something like that," she said, arms still raised.

"Thought you were her mother."

"Happens all the time." Addy forced a snort and a smile.

The rifle had slipped a notch. He straightened it out, steeled his face. "What're you two doing out here? Been following my trail?"

"Passing through is all. Didn't mean you no harm. Saw your horse in trouble. Just wanted to save her."

"And take her, right?"

Addison drew in a tight breath. She nodded, said, "That was our plan. Can cover more ground that way."

"Where is it you're trying to get to?"

"Does it really matter?" She lowered her arms. He didn't object. Her wrist brushed against the Glock. She'd practiced pulling it from the holster and knew she could get a shot off within a second of lifting her shirt. "Take your horse and move on. We'll do the same. Chances are we never cross paths again, so none of this matters. Okay?"

He stood there for several long seconds, tight, rifle aimed at her face.

Addison remained stoic in the face of possible death. Had she reached a point where nothing would faze her? Or was there something about the young man? She knew he didn't want to hurt her, and wouldn't.

He took his finger off the trigger and lowered the rifle. "Maybe I can help you get where you're going."

"You don't need to do that."

"It's all right." The rifle muzzle touched the ground. "Just don't make me regret it."

He walked past Addy toward his horse, casting a glance toward the far off wails of afflicted. He slid the rifle into a loop on the saddle. Then he turned back toward Emma and Addison.

"Funny thing about those—"

"Shouldn't have turned your back on a stranger," Addison said. "Haven't you figured that out yet?"

His stare fixed on the Glock 17 in her hand.

"Now, I want you to take three big steps away from the horse, then get down on the ground. Not on your knees, though. I want you on your belly, lips kissing the dirt."

"Where the hell were you hiding that?"

"Shut up and do what I said."

"You're not gonna do a goddamn thing."

"You really wanna test me?"

He didn't budge, but didn't reply either.

Addy squeezed off a round that sliced through the air above his head and slammed into the tree the horse was tied to. The animal reared up on its hind legs. If they'd managed to untie it, it would have taken off there.

"You crazy bitch!" The guy lifted his hands high and backed away from the horse. "You know what that's gonna do? They're all gonna find their way here."

"Then you better get your ass on the ground so we can get out of here." She nudged Emma. "Go, get her untied."

Emma hurried to the horse. "Whoa, girl, whoa." She gained control of the lead and settled her down. After that she went to work on the knot.

The guy dropped to his knees in a pile of leaves. He looked around the woods.

"On your stomach," Addison said.

"I'm gonna die out here."

She walked over to the horse, never taking her eye or the pistol's aim off of him. "Somehow, I doubt that."

He bowed his back, looked up at her. "You are so gonna regret this."

"Somehow, I doubt that, too." Addison didn't enjoy the exchange, or even what she had done to the man. But he'd brought it upon himself with how he had treated them. She couldn't blame him, of course. It was the way of the world now. She surmised anyone who had lasted this long had learned to be weary of other survivors.

She threaded her left foot into the stirrup and hoisted herself up and over. The few moments she had her aim off the guy weren't near enough for him to get to his feet and regain control of his rifle. She tugged the reins to the left. The horse made a quarter turn, and Addy pulled back.

The shrieks of the dead closed in.

The guy glanced around, sweat on his forehead, fear in his eyes.

For a moment, she felt bad about what they were doing, leaving him there, alone. But he would've done the same.

Rifle blasts thundered through the woods, silencing the afflicted.

He pushed up to his knees, got one foot on the ground. A smile formed as his dark eyebrows knit together.

"I promise you," he said. "You're gonna pay for this."

Addy dug her heels into the horses's ribs and they took off sprinting away. She looked back over her shoulder, over the top of Emma's head, and saw the guy scrambling for his rifle. He was already on it, lifting it up to his shoulder, drawing aim on them. He had a shot, maybe not the best one possible, but he had it. She braced for impact, but it never came. Her head swung forward and back, taking in the terrain ahead and the last glimpses of the man they'd robbed.

She pushed the horse for a mile, at least. Maybe more. Time and distance were difficult enough to track without the adrenaline. They left the woods behind and stuck to a wide road for a short time, remaining off the pavement so the echo of the horse's hooves wouldn't give them away. Every couple hundred yards, she crossed the road, though. Figured if anyone was tracking them, it would be difficult to keep up that way. Asphalt kept no records of those who traveled on it.

Further along, she recognized the area they were in.

"We're not far from Turk's bunker."

"Can we go there?" Emma asked. Addison thought she noticed

a hint of hope in the girl's voice, as though she imagined her father waiting for her.

"I think we should," Addy said. "We could use some supplies after losing that bag in the pit. And Turk said there was a horse farm nearby. Maybe we can find that. Might be easier to make the trek on two horses."

They reached the scorched fields atop the bunker a half-hour later. Addy stuck to the shadows of the woods and scanned the surrounding area. There hadn't been a screech or howl in some time now. Perhaps the lingering smell of fire kept them away, even after time and rain had passed.

She turned her attention to the southeastern sky where black clouds piled up in the distance. A storm clung to the coast. Its winds wove through the trees, wresting the final dead leaves from the branches they clung to.

"I don't like leaving the horse out here like this," she said.

"Seems okay here, doesn't it?" Emma said. "Peaceful."

Addison pointed up at the clouds. "I think it has more to do with that than anything else. Too bad we can't get her down the stairs."

"You want to stay here?"

"If that storm's as bad as I think it is."

Emma ran her hand down the horse's neck. "We can't just leave her out here."

Addison took a deep breath. The air felt thick and wet. "No, you're right. We can't. Let's hurry and then start pushing west. Maybe we can find a house or something off the beaten path."

They left the horse tied to a tree along the edge of the woods, leaving enough line for it to move about. Addison found the opening. She made Emma wait behind as she descended into the ground, her Glock leading the way. She had no fear of using the pistol should someone, or something, get in her way.

At the bottom, amid the soft red glow of emergency lighting, she called out, "Come down, it's clear."

Emma's soft footsteps grew closer. The girl got behind Addy and hugged close to her body. "It's creepy down here."

"Keeps the dead away," Addison joked.

Emma forced a laugh. "I hope you're right."

They reached the sealed door. Addison gave the handle a try. Locked. She pushed on the door. Didn't move. She tugged on it. Same result.

"I thought he left it open," she said. "After he came to get us."

Emma shrugged. "It's all a blur to me. After what happened...."

"I know." Addison threaded her arm around the girl and pulled her close.

"I wish he were here." Emma hung her head. "I miss my dad."

"I got an idea," Addy said. "Wait right here."

She ran down the corridor and climbed the stairs and dropped to her knees in the soft patch of dead grasses and mud. The dampness seeped through the fabric covering her knees. She pulled the grass away and dug into the soil six inches or so to a point where it was especially damp. She scooped two large handfuls out of the ground and headed back to the sealed door.

"What are you doing?" Emma backed away to the wall at the sight of the dripping mud.

"Your dad," she said, "he's a pretty smart guy."

Emma nodded and said nothing while her gaze remained fixed on the mud, which Addy had dumped onto the floor.

Addison shook out her hands. Mud splattered the wall. Some hit both of them in the face. Emma reacted as though an afflicted had spit on her.

"Come on," Addy said. "I know your dad taught you how to live out here."

"Doesn't mean I have to like mud thrown on me."

Addison laughed. Perhaps the first pure laugh she'd had in a while.

"What are you going to do with that?" Emma said.

"Watch."

Addison grabbed a handful and dipped her index and middle fingers of her opposite hand in it. Then she wrote on the door in large block letters: F-A-R-M.

Simple. Effective. And telling.

To anyone who came along, it described the scorched fields above them. But to Sean Ryder, should he ever reach this point, he'd know based on the people who had arrived here. Only one had strong ties to a farm, and that was Addison. And she'd told him enough about the farm and its location that he could find it.

"If—," she stopped, cleared her throat. "*When* your dad gets here, he's gonna see this, and he'll know where you and I are."

Emma blinked at the drying mud. A smiled formed. "He'll know," she said softly. "He'll find us."

They climbed the stairs. Diffused sunlight washed over them. Grey clouds swirled overhead.

Addison heard the horse neighing wildly.

And she froze at the gunshot that followed.

TWELVE

SEAN STARED AHEAD, PAST MEDRICK'S LINGERING GLARE IN THE vanity mirror. He saw the first outlines of what appeared to be a settlement. A razor-wire-topped fence surrounded multiple grey buildings interconnected by covered walkways. Smoke rose from stacks above three of the buildings.

"Seen anything like this?" Medrick said.

The drive took no more than twenty minutes at low speeds. They weren't but a mile or so from the highway. Sean had passed not too far from here a couple of days ago, had no idea what was hidden in the woods.

Had they spotted him then, and tracked him?

It was possible, but it didn't make sense. They'd have come down on him sooner rather than waiting all night.

A man appeared behind the front gate. He threw up a half-salute, ran to the side, and began tugging on a chain which draped across the middle of the fence. The line tightened as he yanked arm over arm. The gate opened up wide enough for the SUV to pull through.

Medrick's window slid down. The man hurried over after securing the entrance. There was a tower about ten yards further down. A man armed with a rifle leaned over the ledge to sneak a peek into the vehicle.

"Anything happen while I was gone?" Medrick asked the sentry.

The man puffed his bottom lip out and shook his head. "Quiet here. Haven't even seen any dead stragglers this morning."

They pulled forward and drove to the left on a gravel road, past the first row of three buildings. There was a large, square structure behind them with high walls and a low-pitched corrugated steel roof. The side they were on had three tall roller doors, with regular doors set in between them. Windows were cut in fifteen feet or so off the ground, six of them. Behind the large building were three more, identical to the first three. A cracked concrete sidewalk ran the length between the outer buildings amid brown grass, dormant for the winter.

Parked near the corner of the lot were four green box trucks and six late-model sedans.

"Bet you folks are thinking you've died and gone to heaven," Medrick said, wearing a shit-eating grin. "Am I right? Or am I right?"

"You been here since the beginning?" Sean said.

"Someone else was here. But they weren't running things the right way. Change of management was deemed necessary."

"What's that mean? You came in and slaughtered them?"

Medrick turned in his seat. "Guy like you, I figure you'd know it doesn't take killing everyone to make a point. Chop off the head, then replace it with your own."

"These guys here, they come in with you? Or were they part of the previous group?"

Medrick stared at Sean for a few moments through narrowed eyes. "You ask a lot of questions."

Sean shrugged and said nothing.

"Why is that? You thinking you want to take this place for yourself?"

"I got no intentions of sticking around here."

"Where is it you think you're going?"

Sean turned to the window and stared past the fence at an open field that led to a hill. "Somewhere else."

"Yeah, well, we'll see about that, friend." The SUV came to a stop and Medrick turned in his seat and opened his door.

The entrance to the nearest building opened up and two armed men dressed in black cargo pants and shirts with vests over them stepped outside and walked up to the SUV. They greeted Medrick in the same manner as the gate guard. He asked for a status update and was told not much had happened, things were peaceful inside.

Sean wondered if something had happened recently that left this guy on edge. Or was he always like that? It made sense to remain vigilant, even when protected from the afflicted the way they were here. Part of Sean hoped that everything back at the cabin was an act, meant to ruffle their feathers. A way of weeding people out. Would Medrick want to bring troublemakers back to a setup like this? Sean sure as hell wouldn't.

Medrick walked toward the entrance and stopped short. He had a radio in his hand. He lifted it to his face and spoke, then waited for a response while staring back at the SUV. He must've got it when his head started bobbing up and down. A few seconds later he disappeared inside.

One of the guards opened up the side door. The man who'd held steadfast with the AR-15 backed out. He never took his aim off of them. If one acted up, Sean figured all of them, including the baby, were dead. This wasn't the time to make a stand. Medrick would have slain them back at the cabin if he had wanted.

First thing that happened when Sean's boots hit the ground

was the man standing next to the passenger door grabbed him by his elbow. The second thing was the guy to his right whacked him across the back of the head with a nightstick.

He dropped to a knee. A warm trickle of blood dripped down his neck and settled into his collar. He placed his hand on the gravel, stopping his torso from collapsing.

"Get up, asshole," the guy said.

Sean turned his head to the side and caught sight of the guy. Silver clouds raced past beyond him. The light that seeped through cast a bit of a halo around the man's head. Or was that a result of a concussion?

The guy grabbed him by his shirt and dragged him along a few steps. Sean couldn't get his feet under him. His hands slipped in the gravel and he went down, face-first. Sharp rocks smacked his right cheek, lips, chin.

Medrick popped back outside. He took a few steps forward, stopped, and said, "All right, that's enough. Get them in. Separate the guys and put the woman in with the others."

"What about the baby?" one of the men asked, as though the child remaining with his mother wasn't something that would happen here.

Or maybe they hadn't encountered it yet. There had to be children inside, though. Right?

"Stays with the mother," Medrick said before heading back inside.

Sean took two steadying breaths, pushed off the ground, and got one foot under him. The world still shone a bit. His head felt a bit like when he got off an extended stay on a boat. He was rocking. His stomach churned. But he made it up without help and soon found a man on his elbow again.

"Just keep walking and don't try anything," the guy said. "You'll make it in, no problem."

The door they went through led to a stairwell landing. A solid brown door was next to the first step. They skipped the door and walked up a flight to another landing, which looked similar to the first, only it had a four-foot high window in place of the exit door. The group stopped here. One of the guards opened the door. But not everyone went through.

Beth and the baby were led away. She looked back at Leo, fighting off sobs until she passed the threshold. Then she let go. Leo looked like he was going to join in as the heavy door slammed shut. The sound echoed throughout the chamber like a shotgun blast.

"Climb," a guard instructed.

Sean took the lead with a man on his heels. Leo struggled below. They were outnumbered by guys armed with rifles and pistols on their hips. The settlement's security force. How many were there in total? They reached the third-floor landing and the man tugged Sean back. A moment later, Leo stood shoulder to shoulder with him. They both faced the door. The guy in front of it rapped his knuckles against the hunk of steel and stepped to the side and waited.

The door groaned open and a jolt of warm air encased Sean. He thought he caught the smell of coffee at first, but something foul overtook it. He couldn't make it out. A cross between used gym towels and sewage, maybe.

The guard at the door spoke back and forth with an unseen woman. Out of the corner of his eye, Sean saw Leo glancing his way for a second or two at a time. Just stay quiet, Sean thought. He didn't want any trouble right here. There was little chance he would make it out alive. Even the uncertainty of what waited behind that door wasn't enough to persuade him to make his move now.

The first thing Sean noticed when the door opened was the

stretch of overhead lights hanging from a high ceiling. They cast soft cones of yellow across a wide walkway. A fan whirred from overhead. Long strands of clumped dust wavered in the forced air blowing from the nearest vent.

The place had power, probably generated on site.

At that moment, as the guards prodded Sean and Leo to start moving to the door, Sean felt a wave of hope wash over him. Maybe these guys weren't that bad. They had something good here, and because of that, they had to go to great lengths to vet newcomers.

The woman who worked the door had hurried ahead a dozen yards or so. She had her black hair pulled back in a ponytail and a green hat sat atop her head. A thick keyring dangled from one hand. Had to be forty keys on it, all bunched together along the bottom and climbing up the sides. She brought her hands up and worked through the keys until she found the one she was looking for. It slid into the lock on the door in front of her. She looked over at them. Her shaded, deep-set brown eyes made her gaze feel hollow.

She pushed the door open and stepped back. Light seeped across the walkway, dominating the yellows cast down from the ceiling.

Leo lurched forward, stumbled and tripped over his feet. He hit the ground like he was sliding into second, face turned away, scrunched up. A man appeared from behind Sean. He walked up to Leo, bent over, grabbed the guy by the back of his collar, and dragged him along until Leo managed to get his feet under him. By the time he did that, they were in front of the room. The guy hauled Leo all the way up, and Sean saw his new travel companion's eyes grow wide. He started to look back. His mouth hung open. He looked scared.

"What the hell? What are you doing to me?" Leo yelled.

The guard shoved him forward. Leo reached out with his hand, grabbing the door frame. The guard slammed the butt of his rifle on Leo's outstretched fingers. The man howled in pain as the last of him slid out of sight.

THIRTEEN

"WHO'S OUT THERE?" EMMA SHRUNK BACK INTO THE SHADOWS until she bumped against the wall. Her eyes reflected the red lighting. The girl bit at her bottom lip. Two upper teeth still too large for her mouth glistened.

The ringing in Addison's ear subsided and an overbearing silence following the gunshot set in. Who was out there? Would they start exploring the area, find the opening? No effort to conceal their descent into the bunker had been made. If whoever was up there decided to investigate the field, they'd stumble upon it.

"I'm gonna check," she said.

Emma lunged forward and grabbed Addison's forearm with both hands. "Don't go, Addy."

"It'll be okay."

"No, it won't. If they find you, I'll be stuck down here all alone."

"And if they come down here, they'll get both of us." She placed her free hand over one of Emma's. "I don't want that to happen."

"I'd rather be captured with you than wandering around alone."

It wasn't the fear of being taken, Addy realized. Emma was petrified of being alone in this world. If only Addy had remained on the boat with Turk. Emma would be there, too, safe and sound. This damned dream of finding her grandparent's farm, finding them alive. She clung to it with every last shred of hope she had, and it was going to get her, and Emma, killed.

One of the men called out. "We know you're out here somewhere. No one would just leave a horse tied up like this." He paused a few beats. "We just wanna help y'all."

Emma looked toward the stairs as though she believed the men. Addison shook her head. She whispered, "We stay right here."

No one could be trusted in this new world, especially not someone who said they just want to help.

They stood with their backs to the door, beyond the wash of dulled sunlight that shone through the opening above. The breeze made its way down on occasion. It filled the space with air that was cool, yet thick and damp. Refreshing, but not.

Several minutes passed without movement or sound from above. Emma had settled down. She slid toward the floor and rested with her knees drawn up to her chest, and her chin on her knees. Her breathing was soft and slow. Had she managed to drift off to another place?

The tension flowing through Addison spiked in her shoulders, stomach, and head. Her pulse pounded, hard enough that it caused ripples in her vision. She wanted whoever was out there to take the horse and go. But if they didn't, the 9mm in her hand, cold against her sweaty palm, provided one last line of defense.

The small tunnel to the bunker door provided a choke point. One where she and Emma couldn't be seen, and a spot where two men could not advance side by side.

Let them come, she thought.

Not too long ago she could have never imagined a thought like that running through her mind. Now she realized in order to survive, she had to stay prepared to fight at any time.

"Over there."

Addison's heart rate spiked when she heard the man. He spoke softly, to someone nearby. She brought the pistol up, held it with both hands, extended it out, aimed it into the muted light. Didn't have to be a perfect shot. Hit them in the chest, stomach, head, whatever, it would stop them and she could finish them off while they writhed in pain on the ground.

She saw movement out of the corner of her eye and glanced over. Emma had risen, sliding up, her back to the door. She pushed her hips forward and retrieved the smaller Glock 19. Damp streaks where tears had slid down her cheeks remained, but that was all. Her face steeled. In the shadows, standing there with the pistol aimed out like Addy, Emma looked a lot like her father.

"You comfortable shooting that at whoever comes down here?" Addison asked.

The girl nodded without saying anything.

"Even if you have to shoot before a word is said between us?"

"I won't let them hurt you, Addy. Just like I know you won't let them hurt me."

"We're a team."

"A team," Emma echoed as she took two small steps and stopped even with Addison.

A shadow shot across the floor in front of them. A moment later, it returned, the length of it stretching from top to bottom. Then it shrunk, as though the guy had lowered into a squat. No doubt to see as far as he could into the tunnel.

"Think they're down there?" a guy said.

The stubby shadow wobbled side to side. "Don't see no tracks leading here or away. Nothing fresh, that is. Grass is matted down going yonder, but that looks old."

"We should check it out anyway. Might be something worth taking down there."

"Yeah, might be." The guy rose as evidenced by his elongated shadow. Then he yelled out, "Stay with the horse."

There were three, at least. Addison figured they were local, judging by the thick low-country accent. The first of them started his descent into what would become his grave if he acted the least bit aggressive toward them.

Next to her, Emma's breath tightened and quickened.

Addison leaned over so their arms touched. It was as much as she could do. No way could she risk giving them away by speaking.

The man's feet and the tip of his barrel appeared first.

Addison closed her eyes, drew in a breath, and opened back up to the world.

His belt came into view. He was almost at the spot where he'd be able to see them, too.

She counted down in her head.

Three.

Two.

One.

The guy had spotted them. He ducked down, knees bending forward, while he drew up his rifle. He intended to shoot first, ask questions later. These weren't good men. Not by any stretch. They came and killed and took what they wanted. Didn't even leave their victims a chance to make it.

Addison hip-checked Emma and the girl fell to the side, into the shadows, out of the man's aim. If he was going to get a shot off, she'd absorb it.

But Addy had no intention of letting that happen. Before the guy even leveled his rifle, she squeezed the trigger. Three rounds exploded from the six-inch barrel. The muzzle blast exploded time and again in her field of vision. The gunshots roared throughout the small cavern. Each landed in a spot that left the man little chance of surviving.

He managed to get off a shot, but it went wide and slammed into the wall next to the door. He dropped his rifle, fell back, slid down to the ground, where the sunlight over his body only lingered for a moment.

The next man was on his way. He yelled something unintelligible, presumably to the third guy who had been instructed to stay with the horse.

"Emma," Addison yelled. She hadn't needed to be so loud, but the loud hum in her ears made it feel necessary. "Are you ready?"

The girl was on her feet and moved into position next to Addison. She squeezed off her first shot the moment the guy's hiking boots appeared. Hell of a shot, too. Nailed the guy right in the shin. He howled something fierce as he drew his leg up. His revolver hit the ground with a thud and skated down the makeshift stairs.

Emma didn't relent. She fired again, hitting his other leg at the knee.

The man collapsed and rolled down to the ground. He came to rest on top of his partner in crime.

Emma drew her aim once more. Addison reached out and pushed the girl's arm down.

"I'll do it," Addison said. "You shouldn't have to."

Emma dropped back into the shadows, beyond the glare of the man who writhed in pain on the corpse of another.

"Anything to say?" Addy said to the guy.

He grimaced hard, then bared his teeth to her. It was obvious the guy relished in the fact oral care wasn't required during the apocalypse.

"Last chance," she said. "Tell me who you are, how you found us."

The guy spat at her, but he lacked the ability to make it count. A little spittle managed to travel a couple of feet and fell in between them. The rest landed on his chin and dripped off the side.

Addison stood five feet away. Wasn't much chance she'd screw up the shot. "If you weren't blocking our way out of here, I'd leave you alive down here to suffer until one of those things sniffed you out and finished the job."

"Screw you, bitch."

That was all she needed to hear. She fired one shot, hitting him in the forehead.

One man left, unless he'd fled. She wouldn't blame the guy. He had no idea what lay in wait underground. A damn army could be down there.

Addison started up the stairs and looked back. Emma hadn't joined her. She stood a few feet away from the two dead men.

"Come on, Em," Addy said.

"I..." It was all she could say. Was she going into shock over having shot someone?

"It's not your fault. Now come on. We gotta see what's going on up there."

Emma did not move.

Addy hurried back down. She bent over the men and hooked her hands underneath the top guy. A few shoves later and she managed to roll him off the first. Then she reached out for Emma's hand. The girl remained in place. Was she going catatonic? God, please let the horse still be there, Addy thought.

"Look girl, I can't move the bottom guy. You're gonna have to skirt around him." Addison's head was moving left to right, looking at Emma, and checking the opening above. She listened for the girl to respond and tried to hone in on someone approaching. She reached down and scooped up the rifle. Might come in handy in a few seconds.

Emma had moved a few feet but stopped again. Her stare was fixed on the first man.

"Come on, get up here behind me," Addy said, louder than she had wanted. But it had the desired effect. Emma shook her head, shifted her stare to Addy, and tiptoed around the guy.

Addison ascended the stairs. The clouds above had parted in the middle. The sun shone down bright. Felt like knives poking through her eyes as she adjusted. She caught a glimpse of the sky. Clouds the color of pewter raced past and that hole closed up about as fast as it had opened.

She thrust the barrel of that rifle into the open air first. A chill started at the nape of her neck and wormed its way down her spine. She hadn't shot that rifle. Didn't even know if the cartridge poking out in front of the trigger had a round in it. The Glock, well, she knew that would do the trick in any situation now.

The guy crossing the field toward her came into focus. She drew aim on him, putting her trust in that rifle. She blinked him into focus. He was young. Bearded. Dark-haired. She'd seen him earlier that day. She'd stolen his horse.

"Put that damn thing down," he yelled.

She didn't. But she did notice that he was walking with his gun aimed toward the ground. Addy pulled her cheek away from the stock. Behind the guy, lying next to the horse, was another man, older, fatter, heavier-bearded. Reminded her of the two dead men in the hole.

The guy stopped a few feet away. He stared down at her. "You okay?"

She nodded and released her right hand from the rifle. It wasn't a gesture of good will. She grabbed her pistol and brought it up.

"I'm not gonna hurt you," he said. "Wasn't going to earlier, either."

"Who...who are you?" Addy asked.

"Jake," he said. "Jake Burge. Not that last names mean shit anymore."

"You with these guys?"

"Hell no." He turned his head and spat with the wind. It traveled a good ten feet before hitting the ground. "I escaped from them. They were tracking me, I guess. Barely managed to get out of sight when they arrived in that glen where you stole her from me. You made enough damn noise they picked up your track."

She lowered the 9mm and emerged from the hole, extending a hand. He grabbed it and helped her out, then dropped to his knees and reached in for Emma.

"What's your name, sweetie?"

"Emma."

"I'm Jake. Good to meet you."

Emma latched onto his hand and scrambled out of the hole and backed away. She threw a cautious glance to Addison, who nodded at the girl in an attempt to ease her mind.

"You could've escaped," Addy said. "They thought you took off on the horse, you could have went in any direction."

"And miss the chance to pay one of those bastards back?" He shook his head. "Plus, those are bad men—" He paused a beat, "—didn't catch your name?"

"Addison. You can call me Addy."

He craned his head to get a view below. "Guess I misjudged you two, though. Looks like you can handle yourselves just fine."

"It's only 'cause they were stupid enough to come down there. If they'd have reached us out in the open, we'd have been caught."

"Where're you two headed?" he asked.

"To her grandparents'—"

Addison placed a hand on Emma's shoulder. "West."

He scratched at his chin and nodded. "Well, I don't really have anywhere to go anymore. I can tag along. An extra set of eyes ain't a bad thing out here."

Addy leaned in and whispered in Emma's ear, asking if she felt okay about the guy. Emma nodded, her eyes never leaving his.

"Okay," Addison said. "There's a horse farm near here. Might have a few left. If we can get there without me shooting you, we'll stick together for a while."

FOURTEEN

Two men forced Sean to take a dozen or so steps. They stopped outside the room Leo had entered and forced him to face the door. Was he to go in next? Sean tried to follow where the woman had gone, but one of the guys grabbed him by the chin and forced him to stare at the door.

Leo's yells turned into shrieks, the kind that make your blood cold and your toes curl under your feet. The only word that could be made out was *no*, and he said it over and over again as the insane cries faded and his voice sounded like water gurgling after it hung suspended in the sink drain.

"Your friend," the guy to Sean's right said, "was not cut out for this place."

Sean ignored him, said nothing.

They yanked on his elbows, pulling his arms wide, and forced him to turn. He caught sight of the woman again. She had walked to the other end of the hallway, where the lights shone a little duller and the dirty floor met a windowless wall.

She fingered through the keyring and stopped on her choice.

The key slipped into the lock and turned without resistance. The door opened up. White light flooded the corridor floor. It seemed brighter than before. Maybe that was due to the lack of overhead lighting at this end.

Sean looked up and saw it wasn't a lack of light fixtures as much as the lights here were burnt out. Maybe there was a shortage and replacing the ones up here wasn't deemed necessary.

The woman peered cautiously into the room between stealing glances at her next victim. She regarded Sean without much thought. Her thin lips remained thin, never turning up into a smile, or folding down in a frown. Her eyes had that disinterested look, the one he'd seen upon countless women in the months after losing his leg. Their gazes would wash over him as though he wasn't there. But they had life in them. This woman had lost all hope of humanity ever returning. He imagined her job would do that to anyone.

The men forced him into position in front of the room, giving him a view of what Leo had seen a few minutes earlier. In each of the far corners were afflicted, one per side. They had ropes tied around their waists. The ropes then threaded along the ceiling, through loops, attached to a pulley. The pulley worked off the door. When it opened, the rope tightened, and the dead were pulled back to their corner, unable to move freely. So when the door was shut again after Sean had been forced in, the dead would be able to move around the room.

The room was an odd shape, Sean noticed. Sort of like a pentagon. The rear wall was pushed back, and at the furthest point, a corner table had been placed. Something sat on top of it.

The woman approached him. She leaned in close. He smelled her, the natural her. There were no fruits or botanicals or Moroccan oil here. Musk and sweat and five days without a shower emanated off her. Had he come across someone like that before all this happened, he'd have turned his nose and moved away. But now, it just was. He found nothing wrong with it. In fact, he thought she was attractive in a way.

She brought her mouth close to his ears and whispered, "All you have to do is retrieve the knife off the table and kill them without getting bit. If they kill you, obviously it's over. But if they bite you and you still manage to dispose of them, well, you'll be hanging out in one of these rooms for a long time to come. If that doesn't work for you, you might just want to drop to your knees and say a prayer to your creator the moment the door slams shut. Sounds like that's what your friend did."

Sean caught her eye as she backed a few inches away. "He wasn't my friend."

She smiled. Sean no longer found her attractive. "I don't care."

He let his gaze move past her, into the room, toward the afflicted. One of them looked like a lost soul waiting for that moment when it would finally be put to rest. But the other, that damned bastard stared at him with those glowing green eyes. Its mouth hung open. Thick strands of mucus and saliva poured over its lips and hung from its chin. It dropped its head back and screeched violently.

"Showtime," one of the men behind Sean said as he planted his hand in the middle of Sean's back and drove him forward.

Sean's gaze swept across the expanding room as he was thrust toward the doorway. The first step caused his makeshift prosthetic to snag on the floor. He reached out and grabbed the doorway to steady himself. Out of the corner of his eye he saw the rifle butt careening toward his fingers. He yanked them away with a second to spare. The buttstock smashed against the frame, denting it. Could have easily snapped his fingers in half, leaving him at a further disadvantage.

"Get in there before I kick your ass in," the guy said. He let go of Sean's shirt. The boot to his back would come in a moment if Sean didn't move.

So he cleared the threshold and stopped there. The door moaned on rusted hinges. Sounded like some of the wails he'd heard escape the afflicted's tormented mouths.

When the door crashed shut, the ropes cutting across the ceiling went slack and drooped like the letter U. Could he use that to his advantage? The ceilings were tall in the corridor. A bit lower in here, but still too high to reach. But he could still reach the dangling ropes.

Sean darted to his left and hooked his wrist around the rope and pulled down, tightening the slack that allowed the afflicted on the left side of the room to approach. The dead was snapped back to the wall. It smacked against it with a thud. Its head fell forward, chin to chest. Behind was a mat of thick, dark blood and strands of hair stuck to the wall.

He remained in place, pressure on the rope, keeping the afflicted trapped, while the other staggered across the room. Its eyes glowed with a faint trace of yellow. Its mouth hung open. A serpentine-like tongue flicked out and to the side, then coiled back into its mouth-hole.

"Come on, you bitch."

The dead continued toward him. Sean waited for it to close the remaining distance with blinding fury.

But it didn't.

The afflicted continued to stagger, almost stumbling over its pigeon-toed feet. They were so distorted that Sean wondered if someone had broken the human's ankles before he turned.

Sean braced his free hand against the wall behind him and shifted his weight so his balance was set perfectly on the tip of his prosthetic. His first hit was delivered by foot when the afflicted had come into range.

A perfect strike to the right knee sent the leg flailing out, and the dead careening face-first to the floor. Sean drove two more strikes with the tip of his hiking boot into its face. Each snapped the head back. Using the taught rope for support, he stepped forward, lifted his prosthetic high, and drove it down through the soft skull. The yellow glow faded.

Sean freed his leg, then stepped over the body, holding onto the rope as long as he could before letting go. He'd reached the middle of the room. The distances between the afflicted and him, and him from the table, were about equal. It all depended on how fast the thing could move.

He sidestepped like a linebacker doing a drill. Instead of instep to instep, he led with his foot, dragged his prosthetic, arms out wide for balance, but ready to strike if necessary.

On the table was a large knife and a hammer. He snatched up both and waited.

The afflicted stopped, tipped its head back, and wailed. The scream tore through Sean's head. He felt it beyond his ears, in his eyes, the roof of his mouth, the base of his skull. The room started spinning. The hand he used to grip the knife went knuckles first to the table in an attempt to help him balance. The table was set a half-foot away from the concrete wall. It slid and smacked into it. Sean lost his footing and fell shoulder-first into the wall.

The afflicted's scream subsided. Its features darkened, if that was possible. The eyes glowed green. It worked its twisted mouth open and shut, only it didn't quite close all the way. The bottom jaw had been smashed at some point and set far to the left. Half its teeth were missing, but Sean knew that didn't matter. All it had to do was get a few in and it was game over, either now, or later. If it ever happened, he hoped it would be instantaneous with full consumption of his brains so that he might never step foot in the world as one of those tortured souls.

Sean regained his footing. He held the knife at his side, blade aimed at the damned bastard still deciding on its next move. The hammer felt heavy and solid in his left hand. He held it so that the head stuck out to the side, away from him.

The afflicted stepped to the side, keeping the same distance between them. It stopped so that it blocked the path to the door. Was it making a tactical decision? Did it realize that when the door opened, it was pinned into the corner?

"How long've you been here?" Sean felt stupid trying to talk to it.

The afflicted's deformed mouth worked open and shut. A garbled and grating whisper escaped. Had it understood? Or was speech a lost relic in whatever remained of its mind, something so engrained it only knew to respond in kind?

Those eyes flashed like bright streetlights changing to green on a pitch-black night. Hands whipped upward, chest high, stretching out. It moved fast and threw Sean off guard. This was the second he'd seen move that quickly in the past twenty-four hours. God help the survivors if there were more like this.

The first step the afflicted took toward Sean was slow and shuffling across the solid floor. The next step was the same. It paused, and if Sean didn't know better, he would have thought it had stopped to grin at him. That decrepit mouth worked open, and that long tongue flicked out, almost sensing the meal that awaited.

Sean spun the knife in his palm, so that the blade stuck out the backside, facing the afflicted. He could slice across his body and sever the rest of the jaw if necessary. He flexed his other arm outward, getting it ready to slam the hammer into the afflicted's temple.

His plan was set. He visualized it while waiting for the damned to make its next move.

Only it didn't do as he expected.

The afflicted dropped its right foot back, flexed the left at the knee, lowered its head so Sean could see the patches of hair that had fallen or been torn out.

Then it charged.

It rushed forward with such speed and force that Sean instinctively rocked backward as though a spear were being hurled at his head. He bowed and dropped his head back as the afflicted advanced through the air. It grabbed Sean's shoulders and its cold, damp body landed on his.

They collapsed back onto the table. Sean's head missed the edge and slipped underneath, while the afflicted was above. It released its grip and started scratching at the tabletop, which had broken free of its legs.

He felt its pelvis dig into his own as it lifted its torso and grabbed hold of the tabletop and flung it overhead. The afflicted let out a loud screech with that mouth twisted open. Its arms moved faster than a professional boxer throwing a knockout punch and latched around Sean's neck.

And it went for Sean's face. Thick mucus fell from its lips onto his own. He slammed his mouth shut against the putrid fluid.

The angles were wrong for an effective attack, but he had to do something, so he punched with his right arm, deliberately missing the afflicted's face by aiming for the air left of its head. The blade went into the vacant darkness of its open mouth and sunk into the decrepit flesh, slicing through its cheeks all the way back to where its jaw connected.

The dead let out a garbled scream as the mucus lining its throat and mouth combined with that sludge-like blood. Sean pulled his head to the side so it wouldn't land in his eyes. The afflicted countered by moving one of its hands up, digging a finger in under Sean's nose and forcing his head back. The strength it possessed was not expected.

Sean found himself staring at the wall behind him. He pulled the knife free, and sliced again, hoping to cut through its throat. A fresh coat of warm blood spilled out and onto Sean's chest.

Then he whipped the hammer through the air with no idea where it would land. He only knew it had when it thudded to a stop. He couldn't yank it free easily after. It took a couple of tries.

Then he did it again. And again. The force with which the afflicted bore down on him eased up, then faded altogether.

He worked his head forward and saw the dead seated on his midsection, arms dropping, chin on its chest. He moved the hammer head to the afflicted's chest and pushed. It fell backward.

Sean snaked his legs out from underneath and got to his knee. He shuffled around to the side and planted the knife into the bashed and battered skull, ensuring that the damned was gone forever.

He remained in the room, back against the wall for what felt like hours. In reality, thirty minutes had passed before the door opened and the woman stepped in.

"You survived. Well done." She tossed him a clean white towel and a bottle of water. "I survived when they threw me in this very same room." She turned away from him and exited, leaving the door open after she passed through. "Come now, before they put the next two in there."

FIFTEEN

THE GENTLE ROCKING AND LAPPING WATER EASED TURK TO consciousness. He had no recollection of the pirates that chased him into the storm that broke the mast that smashed into his head and rendered him unconscious.

He blinked his dry eyes open and immediately slammed his eyelids shut as the sunlight continued to knife through, sending pain throughout his head.

"Turk?" Elana's voice sounded far off, as though he were underwater.

The muted red blur through his clenched eyelids faded to black. He gave it another go and opened up. His eyelids fluttered. Elana sat next to him, one arm stretched over his body. She leaned in and smoothed her hand over his forehead. He felt the cold remains of sweat that must've been there for hours.

He tasted the dried salt on his lips and swallowed hard. His mouth was so dry. When he spoke, it sounded like a frog's croak. "Water."

She leaned over and grabbed a plastic bottle with a faded

white label. The lettering was gone. Probably once said this was the purest water from million-year-old glaciers. Now it was recycled fish piss put through a filter.

And Turk didn't care.

He lifted his head as she put the opening to his lips. A small swallow led to a few large gulps. His throat burned in protest until the liquid put out the flames.

"Do you remember what happened?" she asked as she pulled the bottle away.

He sucked a deep breath in through his mouth. It was warmer than he expected, and not just because of the humidity.

"You know where we are?" she asked.

"On a boat," he said. "The boat we're taking to the island."

She nodded slowly, concern still spread across her face. "Do you remember the storm?"

He closed his eyes and let his head fall back against the stiff pillow. The left side of his skull radiated pain. He reached up to massage it, found a bandage covering a good portion above his ear.

"No, I don't," he said, tracing the bandage. "And I'm guessing this is the reason why?"

"Someone was following us," she said. "Chasing us, actually. There was a storm brewing. I guess you figured it was a thunderstorm, and it might get a little choppy, but we'd get through it."

None of this registered in Turk's mind.

"It was a hurricane," she said. "Or a nor'easter, I suppose, at this time of year. When's the cutoff?"

He smiled at her ability to get distracted even in this environment.

"Anyway," she continued, "you did a pretty damn good job keeping us going through that storm. After we passed the eye, the wall slammed us hard. The mast broke. You took it off the temple like Griffey Jr. was swinging it."

Turk chuckled, which sent more pain through his head. "Everyone make it through okay?"

She nodded. "We're all fine."

"What's the condition of the boat?"

She sighed and looked away. "Not gonna lie, Turk. It's not in good shape."

He closed his eye and bit his bottom lip. How were they going to survive the Atlantic in the winter with no way to navigate and limited food supplies?

"There's good news, though."

"What is it?"

"The guys think we've passed the Gulf Stream and reached the northern stretch of the Bahamas."

Turk planted his elbows into the mattress and forced has back off of it. The blood drained from his head, the pain localized to almost a pin-point while his vision faded to black. He held himself there until he was balanced again. Elana came back into view. She had a slight smile on her face.

"Hey, you're doing better than I thought. Figured you were gonna be down for a week with a concussion."

"You know me better than that," he said. He leaned forward and planted a salty, wet kiss on her lips.

"Want help getting up?" She slid off the side of the bed and stood there.

He waved her aside. "I got this."

Five minutes later, he had rinsed off, swallowed some mouth-wash, and changed into a pair of shorts and a t-shirt. The temperature was in the seventies, and so was the humidity. He didn't care one bit. He climbed the stairs to the deck, craning his head over his shoulder as he hit the open air. All around him the sky was clear blue, the sun shone from high above, and not a cloud was in sight.

Turk lowered his gaze to the crystal blue waters surrounding them. He couldn't believe it. Hours ago—actually he wasn't sure how long he'd been out—the Atlantic had been churning and trying to swallow the battered boat whole. And battered it was, he noticed, as his stare turned inward on the vessel. But they had made it. The final destination wasn't that far away.

Jerry and Alec were at the wheel. Alec took over and Jerry came down.

"You have a nice nap?"

Turk wrapped his hand around the side of his head. "How long was I down?"

"Over a day."

"You're kidding."

"Wish I was."

Turk looked past the man. "I think we found paradise."

"That's what I said when the sun came up yesterday." Jerry followed Turk's gaze out across the turquoise water. "You see it?"

Turk squinted at what he thought might be a land mass. "That an island?"

"Sure is. We've been anchored here for the past day, watching for signs of activity there. Someone's manned the 'nocs the entire time."

Turk checked the deck again and saw one of Jerry's sons leaning against the railing, binoculars up to his face. The steady breeze lifted the teen's hair and tossed it to the side. Every so often he reached up and smoothed it back down.

Gotta keep up appearances, even during the apocalypse.

"So what've you seen?" Turk asked.

Jerry grinned. "Not a damn thing. This might be a good place to pull in, see if we can't repair this old mast and get this thing sailing. And who knows what might be left behind there."

"There's some seven-hundred islands in the Bahamas. Only about thirty are inhabited by more than a family."

"How do you know that?"

Turk chuckled. "Random facts are something I specialize in."

"For some reason, I doubt that."

Turk shrugged and smiled. "What I'm saying is, chances are good we won't run into anyone there, alive or dead. I think you're right, this is a good place to stop." He turned to the side, grabbed the railing and leaned over at his waist. His head spun for a moment or two, and he gripped even tighter.

"All right there, boss?"

"Pull me back," Turk said. His t-shirt tightened as Jerry grabbed the back of it and swung Turk's momentum.

"Thinking of diving?" Jerry smiled, but concern hovered in his eyes.

"Just wondering what the condition of this old girl is."

"She won't sail for shit now. And we're 'bout outta fuel. Should prob'ly have enough to get us up on shore."

"Any chance you circled the island?"

He shook his head. "Figured we'd wait it out over last night to see if any signs of light or fire appeared. Didn't see anything. But, like I said, fuel is low, Turk. We might not make it all the way around the island. Best guess is that we're gonna need to barrel right in and coast to shore, if we can make it that far."

"This is as good a time as any, I guess. Why don't you go and fire her up?"

Jerry nodded and started back up the small staircase leading to the helm.

Layla, who had been watching from the remains of the severed mast, popped out and ran up to her father. He reached down and scooped her up in his arms. She must've looked so tiny as he pulled her into his chest and hugged her.

"You okay, Daddy?" she asked.

"What do I always say?"

"Ain't nothing can hurt my daddy." But the smile that normally accompanied the phrase wasn't there. Her slim eyebrows knit together. "You were asleep for a long time."

"Was a long night, battling that storm."

She fumbled her hand around the side of his head and gently tapped on the bandage. He didn't show any sign of pain, but it hurt when she nudged the wound. "What about this?"

"Flying fish."

Her expression changed and she giggled at the thought. "That's not true."

"It is," he said, lowering her to the ground. Then he brought his hands up and left about three feet of air between. "They were this big. And colored blue and yellow and neon green. They lit up the night for me. But silly me, I got in the way of one, and pow, got me right with his hammerhead."

"Layla," Elana said as she emerged from below deck. "Time for lunch, sweetie."

"But I want to talk to Daddy."

"Sweetheart, he's got some work to do. Come eat and let him be for a while."

She looked up at him with pleading eyes.

He reached for her head and pulled her close again. "Do what Momma says, all right?"

She kissed his cheek and said, "Okay," and ran toward the stairs into her mother's waiting arms. They descended the stairs, hand in hand, Layla disappearing before Elana.

Turk climbed up to join Alec and Jerry up top. Rhea had joined them. She nodded as Turk crossed over.

"Sup, old man," she said.

He laughed. "I'd run circles around you, girl."

"Doubtful." She jutted her angled chin toward the island. "Fancy taking me on in a swim?"

"You know I used to live in the water, right?" After she'd found out he had been a SEAL, Rhea asked him question after question about his experiences. "You wouldn't stand a chance. And if somehow you got ahead of me, I'd drown you." With this, he arched an eyebrow and flexed his chest a little.

"You must've took a harder hit on your head than I thought," she said.

The banter was fun, but they had other things to consider. Turk got down to it. "Jerry told me about the fuel situation. Frankly, it's better than I had presumed. I thought we were bone dry."

"It was luck that one can had rolled out of sight down there," Alec said.

"Got us here," Jerry said.

"Right," Turk said. "And I'd feel a whole hell of a lot better if we could see the other side of that island."

"We'll run out before we get around the tip," Jerry said.

Turk stared out over the open water to the hazy green stretch of land.

"I'm telling you," Jerry said. "We haven't seen any sign of activity. Haven't heard a screech or a wail. I think we'd hear that out here, too."

"Don't you think someone would've noticed you camping out here for a day?"

Jerry seemed to consider this. "Well, sure, but we got here late in the afternoon. They would've needed to be on the beach to notice us before nightfall."

Rhea placed her hand on his arm. "Inhabited or not, this is our only chance to recoup and repair this old girl."

Turk walked past them, up to the rail. He pressed his thighs against it and stared at the island for several seconds. "Okay, we get close, but don't breech just yet. I'll swim up and check it out."

"Then I'm coming, too," Rhea said.

"So am I," Alec said.

He looked back at them and nodded.

While Jerry guided them closer, Turk went to work with a couple of flotation devices, rigging up a system to keep a few rifles dry. He sat Rhea and Alec down to discuss tactics. He kept it simple. Even though Alec had police training, he'd never seen a battlefield.

The engines silenced, signaling it was time to move. Turk gave final instructions to Jerry, hugged his family, then slid into the water, letting his body sink as the warm sea cleansed his wounds. He was never more at home than now. In fact, it was the best he had felt in days. Maybe weeks. He emerged from under and licked the salt off his lips, like he had when he'd come to. He preferred it fresh.

They were on the Caribbean side of the island and out of reach of heavy currents and waves of the Atlantic. The swim to shore took a little time, and not much effort.

"Why didn't we take the raft?" Rhea said.

"The little girls might need it," Turk said. "Not keen on beaching the boat just yet. Might be safer to leave it offshore a hundred yards or so."

"You're the boss," she said before taking a deep breath and submerging her body.

A few minutes later they'd reached shore. White sand stretched from end to end. Beyond the beach, the lush jungle waited. A blessing and a curse, Turk knew. They'd find sustenance in there, but venturing into the unknown was not without risks.

They traveled south along the edge of the jungle. It wasn't long before they came across a water source and a natural alcove that offered shade while capturing the breeze off the water. Banana and coconut trees ringed it.

"Good spot to camp," he said, looking up at the trees. "One of these might work to replace the mast, too. Take a bit of work, but we got the manpower to make that happen."

"Sure do," Alec said.

"Let's continue on a bit," Turk said.

They headed south another ten minutes. The tip of the island was close. That's what Turk wanted to see. What's on the other side?

Instead of navigating around the end, he decided to lead them up a hill. They trekked into the thick vegetation, where the wind faded, and the trapped humid air surrounded them. By the time they reached the top, every member of the group was dripping with sweat.

Turk continued to look for a clearing. Not finding one after several minutes, he found the tallest tree and lashed a webbing of sorts out of thick, flexible vines he'd collected. He wrapped it around the tree and pulled hard, then jammed his feet against the trunk and began walking up.

The view at the top amazed him. He could see out across the Atlantic, rows of incoming waves that crested white as they hit a reef barrier fifty yards out, then reformed before crashing on the shore. The sand wasn't as white, nor as perfect down there. It was strewn with trash and seaweed and driftwood and anything else the ocean could dredge up. He spent five minutes surveying the other side of the island.

A feeling of calm washed over him as he climbed down, almost as serene as those thirty seconds he'd spent underwater after jumping off the boat.

"Well?" Rhea said.

"This is perfect," Turk said. "Let's get the others."

As they descended the hillside, they never knew how close they came to the short man with the bald head who had wrapped himself in the wide leaves of an Alocasia.

SIXTEEN

Addison found one horse left on the farm which had the appearance of an animal that could survive the long trek to Charlotte. She wanted to put the others out of their misery. The paddocks did a fine job of keeping the afflicted out. Someone had gone to great lengths to fortify it. Waist- and chest-high spears impaled the wandering dead. Razor wire in between the blackboard fencing kept those who missed the spears out and dissuaded most humans from attempting to enter.

Those who could find the place, at least.

Nestled in the woods, Turk had only come across it by chance. The directions he'd left with Addy were enough for her to reach it, but she knew no one would seek the stalls out.

The caretaker hadn't made it. The last of the hay had been consumed. There were as many carcasses in the stalls as there were live animals. How had this one, a palomino which she nicknamed Chance, survived?

Their new friend, Jake, had climbed a ladder made from two-by-fours to the loft and found several bags of feed. He fashioned one into a backpack of sorts to take with them. The rest, he opened and spread for the remaining horses. Addison objected. Why let them linger? He countered that maybe someone would come across the stables and be willing to take and protect the animals.

He also mentioned this would make a good place to camp for a while. Addison wasn't sure about a while, but a night there wouldn't do any harm, especially with the outer fringes of a storm passing through. They were protected from afflicted and most living within the fences.

If she had nowhere to go, she could see remaining there through the winter, and then when spring came, see about making it a permanent home.

She lifted her head and watched Emma's frame rise and fall with each of her slow, deep breaths. The girl had fallen asleep the moment her head hit the pillow they'd fashioned out of an empty feedbag and dead grass. It had been a rough day. They had both seen more than enough of the evil side of man. Wasn't it enough they were surrounded by mindless dead who wandered in hopes of finding a living to eat? They now had to contend with people who saw little point in banding together. Rather, they figured this time existed for them to rape and steal and kill.

Addison rose to a sitting position while watching Jake, who leaned back against a post running up to the center of the roof. He didn't react to her moving. She whispered his name. He did not respond. Was this a man who could be trusted? The thought entered her mind and surfaced frequently since meeting the guy. They'd stolen from him, left him stranded in woods full of afflicted. Yet, when he found them, he wanted to do them no harm. He'd tracked them down to rescue them, if need be.

That still didn't make him a good man, though, she told herself. Could all be an act. He could be a sick pervert, worming his way in and then when they let their guard down, they'd see the real him.

The rain eased up, and the heavy thudding against the metal roof eased to something like the sound of snow landing on a frozen surface. The floor underneath the dirty windows illuminated with soft white. Addison walked over to one of them and looked out at the sky. Dark clouds ringed with silver had parted and given the moon a view of the earth. She looked out over the protected fields. The damp dead grass glistened. Some of the afflicted impaled on the fence's fortifications tried to move forward, their arms and legs sagging, their stomachs and chests run-through to the hilt. Others didn't bother. They still had a glimmer of something keeping them animated, but they gave up on progressing some time ago.

At least it seemed that way to Addison.

She hoped she never found out what it was like. It was a thought she tried not to allow to occupy her mind. The kind of thing she could spend hours lost in, wondering what it was like to wander the earth with no purpose, no reason behind each change of direction. In a simple way, there was something animalistic about them. But she knew it was more than that. The evil in their eyes and actions could not be written off by calling them scavenging dogs. The dead had a purpose and that was to hunt the living.

Addison turned around and went back to her resting spot, but she didn't lay down. She watched the other two while feeling something pull at her. Jack *was* a good guy. It was more than a notion. He could've run, but he came to save them.

Would he take care of Emma if she left right now?

She gathered a few things together and placed them by the ladder, then shuffled across the floor to where the girl lay sleeping. The plywood creaked with every step. She dropped to her knees. Emma's body rose and fell with her breaths. A smile played on her lips for a few seconds, then faded. Perhaps she was dreaming of better times spent with her mom and dad. Maybe it was just muscles firing for no reason at all.

As she looked down at Emma, Addison told herself she owed the girl nothing at all. She hadn't invited her to come along. She let her tag along because, what else was she supposed to do? Immediately her fears that Emma would slow her down were shown to be true.

Another part of her brain countered that they never would have found the horse in the woods had Emma not been there. And, while that was true, they also wouldn't have gone back to the bunker to find supplies that had been lost. Addy would have found the stables and a suitable horse and been on her way how she had wanted.

Alone.

She worked her finger under matted strands of hair on Emma's cheek and tucked them behind her ear. The moonlight stretched across the floor, illuminating the girl for a moment before racing clouds blocked the light again.

"You take care of yourself," Addison whispered. Then she kissed her fingertips and brushed them against Emma's cheek. Her skin still had that childlike softness. That was probably all that remained of the girl who existed before the outbreak.

Addison rose and crossed the loft, stepping softly to no avail. The flooring creaked with every step, no doubt louder to her ears than anyone else's. She reached the ladder and tossed her things down. They hit the ground with soft thuds. Didn't seem to disturb the animals below. She turned to take one last look at Emma.

"Jesus!" She threw her arms up, fist balled, ready to strike.

Jake grabbed her wrists to keep her from attacking.

"Let go of me." She reversed the grip and gained control of his wrists, then kicked him in the shin.

"Dammit," he said. "The hell are you doing?"

"I told you to let go of me."

"I was just trying to keep you from hitting me." He took a couple staggering steps back and reached down to rub his lower leg. "Where are you going?"

"Out."

"Oh, like for a drink or something, huh?"

She stood there silent, glaring at him.

Jake pointed back at Emma. "Just gonna dump her on me? That's your big plan? You take off and expect I'm gonna take care of her?"

"Basically."

"What is wrong with you? You don't even know me? I could be a damn killer."

"Then I guess I'm right in getting away from you."

"No way you'd leave the girl behind if you thought that."

"I..." She took a deep breath and let her shoulders slump. "I don't know what to think." The resolve that had been there moments ago to take off without Emma and never look back had dissipated.

Jake walked toward her, keeping his body angled to be a smaller target in case she decided to attack a second time.

"I'm not gonna kick you again," she said.

"I know you're not. You're armed, though. Really not sure about taking this chance." His voice was stern, but in the returning soft moonlight, she saw his slight smile. "Look, I know it's tough out here. I started off with my brother and pa. Lost my bro first. Dad couldn't handle it, got weak. Died shortly after. I was alone for months after that until those assholes scooped me up one night. I finally got away, then had the good fortune of running into you."

Addy glanced over at Emma and thought about telling Jake he had her to thank for his misfortune in the woods. "You could've taken off after we left."

"I couldn't leave you to face those guys alone."

"I think we did all right." She put her hands on her hips and straightened. "Took two of 'em out."

"And the third would have blown a hole in your head the moment you popped up from underground."

"If you hadn't been there," she said softly.

"Where I'm from, that makes us a team."

She considered asking him where that was, exactly, but opted not to.

He continued. "You don't have to go this alone. I'm here to help you. Help you get where you're going and help out with the girl. Together we can do this. You're strong, Addison. I sense that already."

She stood in the same spot, her voice choked in her throat.

He lowered his shaking head before turning around and saying, "If you gotta go, then go. I'll make up something to tell the girl."

She felt the first tear spill down her cheek. Several more followed. Jake had walked back across the loft and laid down in the same spot. He covered his face with his arm, not bothering to watch Addy make her decision. She shifted her gaze back to Emma. The girl hadn't moved. She hadn't witnessed the encounter. She wasn't forced to see Addison crying because her mind had already been made up.

The two-by-four felt rough against the bottoms of her fingers as she grasped the top rung of the ladder. She worked her way down without looking back. The air on the ground level felt stifled and smelled like a half-dozen horses lived down there, which was about right. She entered the stall of the healthiest and prepared it to leave.

The sun would be up in an hour or so, but Addy didn't want to wait it out. Too much time to think and change her mind. She had to go.

A stiff wind chilled her as she stepped out of the stable into the night air. The clouds had thinned even more. The moon hung low and glowed pale blue. She investigated the perimeter of the paddock, stopping at the gate to make sure the path was clear and there'd be no problems locking up after she went through. There could be no what-ifs, and walking away while wondering if she'd left the other two to die would linger on her mind forever.

The area was clear of afflicted, and the gate would be no problem from the outside. Addison returned to the stable, gathered her supplies, and led the horse away.

SEVENTEEN

T<small>HE ROOM THEY SHOVED</small> S<small>EAN INTO WHILE HE WAS STILL COVERED IN</small> the rotten blood of the afflicted he had slain was dark and damp and smelled like piss and shit. The odor of human waste stunk so badly he couldn't smell the dead on him anymore. Worst of all, he'd almost adapted to the odor in the small room.

The floors were concrete and covered in dust. The walls were solid, too. Water ran down them in trickles. He wasn't sure if that's how they expected him to hydrate, but upon close inspection, there was a strong hint of sulfur. He cupped his hand on the wall long enough to fill his palm half-full repeatedly, using the accumulated liquid to wash the remains from his hands and arms and even his face, though he was careful not to drink any.

A day and a night had passed since they cast him aside. His stomach knotted with hunger, a sensation he knew would go away in time as his body adjusted and turned to stored fat for fuel. He spent his time doing pushups or squats or attempting to meditate. It didn't come so easily to him, and given the circumstances, this wasn't the best place to cement his practice.

One thing that did not happen was sleep. Once the dark set in, the cries turned up. Whether the pained wails of the afflicted, or those living who had been cursed to live out their days in the confines of the settlement, they howled from one corner or another from within the building.

He figured this was the prison ward. Why else put him through a trial by afflicted where losing meant death and living resulted in confinement.

What had the woman told him? She'd survived, too, something like that. So perhaps making it through the trial meant you earned a position on staff.

"Whoop-dee-fucking-doo," he whispered. His words climbed the corner to the ceiling and died there.

He thought of Leo, and the painfully abrupt end to his life. It was coming one way or another, that much Sean was sure of. He'd lied to Medrick and his men about the wound on Leo's arm. An afflicted had bit him. The sickness had set in, as evidenced by the layer of sweat always present on the guy's forehead. Didn't matter if he was standing in the frigid air, his head glistened. Sean was ready to do what was necessary, but wanted Leo to see for himself his sister-in-law and the infant had survived.

Still, being ripped apart and eaten by two afflicted was no way to go. Did they know they were killing someone who'd already been bit and was turning? Probably didn't matter, it wasn't like the dead stopped feasting on a living being after the first bite.

Did they stop the attack? Would Leo be the next to find himself strung up in one of those rooms, roaming the floor until the door opened and drew him back into a corner, fresh meat about to be forced in to take him on?

Sean felt guilty for having not told Medrick Leo had been bitten. Could've saved the guy's soul the pain of knowing how he died. Then again, seeing how they used the afflicted here, they probably would have bound and gagged Leo and brought him along, leaving him alone in a cell until he passed, then dumping him in a room as he reanimated.

He stretched along the floor and did a set of fifty push-ups to distract his mind from everything that had happened in the past two days. As he completed the set, the door to his room opened and a swath of light washed over him.

The woman from before entered. Her dark hair spilled down over her shoulder. Gone was the hat that had adorned her head. She was dressed the same. In her hand dangled a 1911. She didn't seem intent on aiming the pistol at him.

"Ready to get cleaned up?" Her gaze never settled on him, it bounced overhead, to the side, but never *on him*. It was as though she lived in another dimension. Hell, the idea wasn't as far-fetched as it sounded. Who knew what she had seen in the time following the outbreak.

Sean pushed off the floor and used the wall to steady himself as he rose on his good leg. "What's your name?"

She shrugged. "Medrick calls me his special one, though I suppose he says that to anyone with tits." Her stare finally fell on him, his face first, then to his chest. "Doesn't appear you have that problem."

Sean found himself smiling at the woman. A smile that she didn't return.

"I'm Sean," he said.

She nodded before turning away. "Better hurry, this door won't stay open long."

He crossed the small room and caught the door with his foot before it closed. The heavy hunk of wood hit him with a thud. He drove his shoulder into it and eased out into the corridor. She waited alone ten feet away. They continued side by side once he caught up to her.

"How long've you been here?" he asked.

"Long enough to see most of them die."

"Most of who?"

"Those I arrived with."

"Friends? Family?"

"Just people I found after it happened. We banded together, sort of. Were found some distance from here. Brought here. Lived and died here."

"How many did you travel with?"

"Some would consider it lots. Others maybe not so much."

"You're very straightforward," Sean said, shaking his head.

She said nothing in response. The end of the hallway approached. She pulled out her keyring and began sorting through them, landing on a green colored key with a yellow Packers logo on it. She unlocked the last door and led him in.

The door opened up to a wide room with tile flooring and locker-lined walls. Two rows of benches anchored to the floor created a walkway down the middle. A waist high wall stretched from either side, leaving a gap of about four feet in the middle. Dirty chrome shower heads extended from the far wall.

She shut the door and locked it, then pointed toward the showers. "Strip and wash."

Hanging over one of the short walls was a white towel. Perched next to it Sean saw an unwrapped bar of soap, maybe halfway used. Upon closer inspection, there were curly hairs left behind, caked into the soap. He glanced back at Medrick's Special One. She remained in the same spot, arms at her side, 1911 dangling again.

"Strip and wash," she said again, only this time her gaze settled upon him.

He peeled off his soiled clothing. The skin underneath wasn't what you would call clean, but it looked like it compared to his exposed skin. He walked into the open shower stall naked. The cool air washed over him. Nothing compared to the frigid spray that erupted from the nozzles when he cut the valve on. He took a few steps back and waited in the mist.

"It won't get much better," she said. "We can have hot water, or we can have lights. Medrick says lights, though he gets both in his private room."

He didn't bother asking how she knew, instead tossing her a nod as he grabbed the soap and braved the arctic waters. The cold hit him with a ferocity he hadn't felt in years. After adjusting and loosening his throat to gulp down a breath of air, he rinsed the hair off the bar, lathered up, and washed off, growing more accustomed to the cold with every passing second.

"Okay," she said. "That's long enough."

Sean used the final seconds to rinse thoroughly, then cut the water off. Drips slid off the showerhead and splashed in the dwindling pools on the floor.

"Better?" she asked.

"Mostly," he said.

She moved to the right, stopping in front of a locker. She gave him another once over, then moved two lockers down. There was no lock to deal with. She opened it up, pulled out a pair of dark underwear, heavy khaki pants, two shirts, one short- and one long-sleeved, and a pair of boots. She held both in her hands for several seconds, staring at his naked legs.

"It's all right," Sean said. "One'll work for me."

She nodded, closed the locker, then gathered up the items and set them on a bench. Sean approached with the towel draped over his arm, covering the front of his body. The woman turned and walked to the door, where she stood facing away from him.

"Get dressed now. He's waiting."

Sean would've found her behavior odd at that moment, had she not said those last two words.

"You taking me to see Medrick?" he asked.

She ignored the question. "Are you dressed?"

He pulled on his pants and tugged down the second shirt before sliding his foot into the boot. They'd removed the laces. Guess they figured he might use them as a weapon. "Yeah, let's go."

She led him across the hall to a small door that opened up to a narrow stairwell with flights running up and down. The former must've led to the roof or a rooftop maintenance shack, as they were on the top floor. Sean looked up and spotted the sunlight seeping past the edges of the hatch. How many guards were up there? The roof provided a great vantage point. Medrick would take advantage of that. By keeping guards on the perimeter of each building, just out of sight, he could watch over several acres and see an enemy coming before they realized what lay ahead.

They trotted down two flights. At the bottom landing, a brown door with a small window cut into it about head-high opened up to a courtyard with a long concrete walkway. Dead grass poked out in the seams every six feet.

The cold air didn't affect Sean, underdressed as he was. But it bit at his head under his damp hair.

They walked in the shadows behind the central building, what appeared to be a large warehouse. There were no windows back here offering a view inside. Every twenty feet they passed a door, barely noticeable at any kind of distance. Even the handles were painted to match the facade.

They turned right when they reached the end and continued down a walkway, until about halfway, then made a left. The middle building on this side stood a floor shorter than the ones bordering it. The woman led Sean up to the double doors and stopped there.

He glanced above the doorway and noticed a camera set off to the left, aimed down at them. Footsteps from inside grew, and so did the anticipation. He took a deep breath, steadying his heart, and reminded himself that if they had wanted him dead, there's no reason to have wasted water letting him wash up first.

A tour or a meeting was going to take place. They wanted something from Sean. What, though? Information? Were they curious what he had seen in his time out in the new world? Did they want locations of camps they could invade?

The door on the right opened and a man armed with an HK MP7 brought his free hand up to his forehead to shield his eyes from the bright sun.

"What happened to the storm clouds?" he said.

The woman tilted her head. "You want the rain? This place gets so messy when it pours."

"Just an observation, T."

She shot a quick glance at Sean, then returned her gaze to the man. "Is he ready to see him?"

"Almost. Finishing something up. Come on in out of the cold." The guy took a step back. His posture relaxed after he eyed Sean up and down. "How long were you out there?"

It took Sean a moment to realize the guy was talking to him and wasn't referencing their time in front of the building.

"Since shortly after it happened," he said.

"Hide out for a while?"

"Something like that." He would offer up as little as possible without being too arrogant about it. That always brought about a determination on the interrogator.

"Guess a lot of us took that route. Seemed those who rushed out, or panicked amid all the confusion, ended up dead." He paused a beat and shook his head. "Or worse, wandering around eternally damned to remain on this earth."

"Preach," the woman said. Sean noticed a small smile on her face. Her sense of humor, what there was of it, surfaced.

"All right, lemme check if he's ready." The guy turned on his heel and strutted down the hall to the far end where a set of double doors stood.

"What's going on?" Sean asked. "And what does T stand for?"

She took a quick look at him, sighed and turned toward the door. She stopped with her hand covering the knob and looked back again. "Wait here. If I see you again, I'll answer your question."

The uneasiness that raced through him at hearing the word *if* sent Sean reaching for the wall to steady himself as though she'd swept his wooden prosthetic out from under him. The hell was this place? And who was Medrick?

"Come on," the guy called from the end of the hall. The strap to his MP7 stretched tight as he extended the firearm out with one hand while gesturing with the other.

Sean pushed away from the wall and made his way down. He couldn't see much beyond where the guy stood. The room past the doors was dark. When he reached the man, he saw why. A solid wall three feet behind the doors blocked the room. It was made of metal and spray painted black. A shield, maybe, to protect the person behind it. No doubt constructed after the outbreak.

"Go on in," he said. "Right or left, don't matter."

But Sean figured it *did* matter. He'd seen enough of Medrick to think the guy probably had a profile ready based on which way Sean entered. So he stuck to the left, figuring most would go right.

As he eased around the corner he saw Medrick seated behind a wide wooden desk, the kind a lawyer might use. The smooth surface held no clutter, just a mug with the slogan "I See Stupid People" holding some pens and a highlighter. A yellow legal pad laid out in front of Medrick, the top page covered in scribbles and doodles. Sean spotted what looked like an afflicted in the upper left corner, eyes glowing pink, the color of the highlighter.

"Well, if it isn't Peg Leg Pete," Medrick said. He clapped his hands together and dropped his feet off the desktop. "Excuse me if

I don't stand. Don't know why that seems rude to me, considering you only got that one pitiful leg there." He gestured toward the red vinyl seat opposite him.

Sean stood in place, four feet from the chair, in the middle of the room. "Name's Sean."

"Of course it is." Medrick leaned back in his chair. He made a production of crossing his left leg over his right, lifting his foot high in the air. "Come on, sit. I don't want to have to tell you again."

Sean glanced to both sides, taking in the room while he walked toward the chair. There wasn't a whole lot in there. Some empty bookcases. A small refrigerator that gave off a distinct hum. The thing that caught his eye were two swords mounted to form an X.

"You like my swords, huh?" Medrick leaned forward. "I keep hoping I get a chance to use them. Well, sorta. That'd mean the fence was breeched and we got us a horde of a problem."

Sean spun the chair, eased into it and swung back to face the other guy. Medrick slapped his hand on the desk.

"You want a beer?"

This caught Sean by surprise. "A beer? Seriously?"

"Serious as shit, my one-legged friend."

Sean tried not to shake his head at the remark. Tried unsuccessfully. "Yeah, I'll take one."

Medrick hopped up and walked over to the fridge. Not once did he glance back at Sean. Might have had something to do with the two swords in front of the guy. He pulled open the fridge and grabbed the empty end of a six-pack ring. Dangling from his grasp were two blue cans of Bud Light.

"Not the best stuff in the world, but damn it tastes good these days." He tore a can free and tossed it overhead to Sean, who reached up and snagged it out of the air. "Nice catch."

"Thanks. I passed first grade PE with honors."

Medrick stopped short of his desk, looked down at Sean and cracked a smile. His teeth were too white.

Sean lifted the can to his lips and took two long pulls from it. The bitter taste gave way to the carbonation burn in the back of his throat. A feeling he thought he'd never experience again.

"I'm intrigued by you, Sean," Medrick said.

"Why's that?"

"I'll get to that, but first I gotta know." Medrick drummed his fingertips on the desk for a few moments, building up a little suspense. "Do you want to live or die today?"

EIGHTEEN

AFTER SPENDING THE NIGHT ON THE BOAT JUST OFFSHORE OF THE island, Turk brought his group to land. He waited on shore at the location he'd selected for a camp while Rhea ferried them in on a raft. Elana and the children were last to arrive. He took her on a tour of the surrounding area.

"You feel we're okay here, babe?" she asked, once they were some distance away from the others.

"I feel good about it. Haven't seen another boat since we arrived. No activity on the island. We're a good distance from Florida, so maybe people aren't venturing out this far with gas supplies being limited as they are."

"But there were people out to hurt us near Charleston."

"Yeah, and we weren't that far from shore. They probably had reserves stored somewhere. A hideout on land." He lifted her chin and looked her in the eye. "Might've been opportunists who came across us while fishing and decided to take a chance."

She nodded and said nothing.

"Gotta trust me on this one. We're good here." He took her

hand and started back toward the others. "Besides, we're not staying long. Everything we need to repair the boat is here. Four days, max, and we're on our way. You can lead the kids on a mission to gather up as many coconuts and bananas as you can find. That'll come in handy as we make our way to the Exumas."

"Then we can start rebuilding."

"That's right. We'll be a force when combined with the others, and we can start going island to island, clearing out the afflicted, finding the right people. We're gonna take back the world."

"That's my Turk," she said, resting her cheek against his shoulder. "Planning on saving everyone."

The group spent the day prepping the site. They set up temporary shelters, which were nothing more than sticks and leaves, but offered the various groups within the group some privacy. After the kids played on the beach, Elana and Jerry's wife took them to collect food for dinner.

Rhea brought the water distillation kit from the boat and rigged up a system that diverted fresh water from the stream into it on demand. She employed Jennie and Sarah to help. There were smaller rafts on board that they used as bladders to hold gallons of water.

Alec and Jerry's kids fished from shore, bringing in a nice haul of snapper and bluefish. Jerry rigged up a fire pit and fashioned a grill set a few feet over the anticipated height of the flame. That way it would cook the fish thoroughly without charring it.

As the day wound down and the sky streaked orange and pink and purple, Turk looked at the group that had grown into a family and now gathered around. People were talking, sharing, laughing. For a moment, he forgot about the tragedy that had befallen the world.

This was the kind of place he could see returning to after they'd done the work. The work that would lead to restoration. He and Elana could retire on this island. It had everything they needed.

Long before the outbreak, this had been one of his dreams. Heading down to the Caribbean and getting lost, him and his wife, rediscovering their love for one another while cutting off from the connected world.

He looked across the circle at her, saw the young woman he fell in love with in the late afternoon light. Out of the corner of his eye, he spotted Sarah running along the coastline. She sprinted the remaining distance to the group.

Hunched over with her hands on her knees, she caught her breath, then said, "I can't find Jennie."

Rhea stood. "I thought she was with you?"

"She was," Sarah said, casting a quick glance at the younger girls, who had gone still. Young Paige's eyes were wide and growing wet. "We were foraging a bit, and I headed down a path, told her I'd be back. And when I returned, she was gone."

Turk stared across the campsite at Elana, who was watching him. He gave her a nod.

"All right, Jerry, you and your boys stay here and watch over the place. Alec and Rhea, come with me and Sarah." He touched her arm. "We'll start at the spot you got separated."

"I'm so sorry, Turk," she said. "It's all my fault."

"No, it's not. Just relax. It's easy to get disoriented in a thick jungle. Trust me, it's happened to me before, and I had years of training." He pointed at Jerry. "How many flashlights did we bring?"

"Four," he said.

"All right, you keep two, we'll take two."

"Got these emergency whistles, also."

Turk went over and inspected them. There were three, orange in color, hanging from matching paracord lanyards. He tossed one to Jerry and gave the other to Rhea. "Here's the deal. One long whistle means something is wrong. Two whistles means we found her, three means Rhea and Alec found her, and four means she made her way back to camp. Got it?"

Jerry and Rhea repeated what he'd said. Turk nodded and motioned for the predetermined parties to follow him away. He waited until they were far enough from camp to speak openly.

"You didn't hear anything when this happened?" he said to Sarah.

"No, but I wasn't really paying attention, either. I mean, we're all alone out here, right?"

Turk stared up into the jungle. His gaze turned upward as it sloped with the hillside, a spine that ran through the center of the island.

"I'm not sure anymore."

Alec looked back over his shoulder. "Are they safe back there?"

"Jerry's got it. Him and his boy are a formidable defense."

Alec didn't look convinced.

"I left my wife and daughter there, didn't I?"

"Suppose so," Alec said. "Just a little spooked."

"Look, I'm programmed to think the worst so that I'm prepared for it. Chances are she wandered off and lost her way. Probably on the other side of the island wondering why she's seeing waves coming in and wondering where our camp is. Or she's up top there somewhere." He pointed over the tree line. "Waiting for the sky to darken and the campfire to guide her back."

"Speaking of the dark," Rhea said. "How far are we?"

"Half-mile, maybe," Sarah said. Then she yelled out, "Jennie!" The gentle breeze carried her voice away, and the thick vegetation threw it back in a series of echoes.

They hurried along at a steady clip. A few minutes later Sarah pointed at a break in the jungle.

"We entered there," she said. "A path heads up the hill a bit."

"Lead the way," Turk said.

The shadows deepened twenty feet in and they switched on their flashlights, scanning the ground ahead for obstacles. Sarah stopped a couple of times. The encroaching dark was making it difficult for her to determine where they had split.

"Around here," she said. "Somewhere. It looks so different now."

Turk understood. "That's the danger in a place like this. It closes in, swallows you up, then changes on you."

Sarah continued forward another twenty feet. She turned in a circle, shining the light around. "Here. It was here."

"You sure?" Turk asked.

"I remember this." She waved the light back and forth. "See how the path splits in four directions? I went down there." She extended her arm and the flashlight out to the right.

Turk met her at the spot and scanned their surroundings. "So she didn't go that way. And chances are she didn't head down to the beach, or if she did, she'll realize at some point she turned the wrong way."

"Or she'll continue all the way around the island," Rhea said.

"And she'll end up back at camp," Turk said. "So that leaves two possibilities. Rhea, you and Alec head down there." He pointed off in the opposite direction of the path Sarah had taken earlier. "Sarah, come with me. We'll head up the hill."

As they climbed, Turk glanced back often. He could see the white of their flashlight through the vegetation at first. It faded quickly, though, as the jungle swallowed them whole.

"You think she's up here?" Sarah said.

Turk shrugged, then realizing she probably couldn't see the gesture, said, "She could be anywhere. Good thing for us this is a small island."

"Small enough you should hear someone call out your name from anywhere on it?" Sarah stopped and grabbed his forearm. "She never called back, Turk. I'm worried something happened."

He realized then that the seedling of that thought had germinated on the beach. It was a small island. But small enough to hear someone yell from any point on it?

"You've got the hill to contend with," Turk said. "The competing breezes, too. One sweeping in from the Atlantic. The other from the Caribbean. Sound only carries as far as resistance lets it."

Sarah nodded, but in the dim light, he saw she wasn't convinced.

"Come on," he said. "Let's get to the top and yell for her up there."

Ten minutes later the effects of the humidity and lack of wind had kicked in. Sweat coated Turk's forehead, chest, and back. He wiped a thick layer off his brow. It dripped off his finger. They found a clearing at the top of the hill. From it, the sun set into the sea behind them, the tip finally dipping into the water, painting it in deep purple.

"Should I call for her?" Sarah asked.

"Good a place as any," Turk said.

She screamed out, "Jennie!" and received no response.

The seconds turned into minutes. They stood there as the island's insect population overtook the silence.

"Wonder how the other group is doing?" Sarah said.

Turk didn't answer. He was staring down into the east-facing side of the hill.

"What's wrong?" she asked after he switched off the flashlight.

"The hell you think that is?"

"What?"

He stepped in close to her so they could both see down his arm and extended finger.

"See those twinkles through the leaves?"

"Twinkles? Where?" Sarah drew in a sharp breath. "Are they moving?"

They sure as hell were. He slid his pistol from the holster tucked inside his waistband. Sarah glanced over, then did the same. She mimicked his posture, both hands on the firearm, extended out, but aimed at nothing in particular.

"Turk, is someone out there?" She glanced over at him, then back at the trees. "They are moving."

"Keep your voice down," he whispered. "We're gonna move back into the jungle, okay? But I need you to be my eyes. One hand on my shoulder, squeeze to stop me."

She turned, placed her hand on his shoulder, and then they moved in unison. He kept his pistol up. The lights had increased in both number and brightness. What the hell was going on here?

Sarah's fingernails dug into the flesh on his shoulder, deep enough they might've drawn blood.

"What is it?" he whispered.

She didn't reply.

A loud shrill whistle tore through the buzzing air. The insects went silent. Felt like the distress call went on for hours. It hadn't faded into silence for five seconds before another whistle, this time closer, cut through the stillness. Again, a single long whistle.

The one he'd instructed the group to use when there was danger.

At once, the clearing lit up. Lights strong enough to blind him blasted at them from all directions. Turk lifted his free hand to his brow in an attempt to see through the brightness.

"Drop your weapon," a man called out.

Turk stood there, pistol extended. Sarah butted up against him, her back against his, their sweat blending.

"We have you outnumbered fifty-to-one, and we are all armed," the guy yelled in an accent Turk couldn't discern. Almost sounded robotic. "If you want to not die, I suggest what I say you do."

NINETEEN

ADDISON PUT TWO HOURS BETWEEN HER AND THE STALLS WHEN THE memory of staining the bunker door with mud arose. She'd written the word farm, big and bold, so that if Sean reached South Carolina, he'd know where to go next.

And she could feel it to her core that he'd decipher the message without a problem. The connection had been made between the three of them.

How could she face him at her grandparents' farm, knowing she'd left Emma behind with a stranger? He'd look her in the eye, eyes that pleaded to see his little girl again, and she would have to tell him she snuck out in the middle of the night like a coward, not even telling the girl she'd left.

Addy had stopped for at least ten minutes. She couldn't go forward. Couldn't see through her tears.

So she made the decision to return. Not to the stables. No, she'd made up her mind that the only way forward was alone. The responsibility bore down on her with such a weight she couldn't breathe half the time.

Addison would go back to the bunker and wash away the message so Sean would never attempt to come find her at the farm.

For a moment, she hated herself for being selfish. The feeling led to rage. She hadn't asked for this. Not to survive. Not to be saved. Not to be brought in as part of a family. She hadn't asked Emma to join her on her journey.

"It's not my responsibility!" she yelled.

A chorus of crows who had lingered in the woods rose into the air and joined her with a cacophony of caws. The whole lot of them darkened the sky above her, almost as if they were a harbinger.

Don't go back, she heard in their calls. The road to salvation is paved with blood, they said. Only to Addison, the blood extended in all directions, yet salvation did not linger beyond the horizon for most. Maybe salvation waited in the bite of an afflicted. The truly lucky would find their souls ripped from their fleshy tombs entirely. But others would not be so fortunate. They'd be trapped in their cages, unable to control the urges to hunt and kill their fellow man.

After resting for a short time, Addison turned her horse around and made her way back. She'd stuck to the highway on her journey out for the most part, keeping it just in sight through the veil of trees. Now she rode in the open on the stretch of dead grass that buffered the living forest from the cold dead asphalt.

Hundreds of cars lined the roadway. Long abandoned and most likely cleaned out. She slowed to investigate a few along the way but found little of interest. There were more dead bodies than anything.

She tried to imagine the scene when all of these vehicles had become stuck. It had to have been early on, people evacuating Charleston. A good portion of them would have been tourists, enjoying a late summer vacation at the beach. Probably had been filling their bellies with low-country cuisine when the first images of the afflicted appeared on television. Maybe they had family or pets or friends and neighbors to get home to. Maybe they figured they were safer in their own houses.

Their assumptions were right. They acted on them too late.

The lack of afflicted disturbed Addison. Even though the traffic jam had occurred months earlier, there should be some dead lingering in the area.

Was it the storm? Had it sent them away? She considered it, and the thought that lingered in the forefront of her mind was this: Where could they have gone?

From what she'd seen, the afflicted weren't the brightest group, and they moved with the speed of a sloth most of the time, with the exception of when they attacked. Maybe they smelled blood when they got within a certain distance, but once their hands were on you, it was game over for most.

She spotted the sign for the exit nearest Turk's bunker and slipped back into the woods. The sunlight diminished and the sweat on her body chilled her to her core. She hopped off her mount for a few minutes and led the horse by the reigns until she warmed up, then got back on.

The path ahead wasn't clearly marked. She had to reach the second road that cut through the woods, then follow it for about a half-mile, then travel through open pasture. The remaining journey took less than twenty minutes.

Her final approach took her in from the opposite direction she and Emma had arrived the day before. As she closed in on the final hundred yards, she heard voices in the distance. They rose and fell, undistinguishable and indecipherable.

Addison tugged on the reigns. The horse stopped, batting its head left, then right. Stomping one of its hind legs in the dirt twice. Addy leaned over, feeling the coarse mane tickle her neck and chin.

"What is it?" she whispered.

The horse took a few steps back.

Someone laughed in the distance. Someone else yelled something. The words were too hard to make out, but the tone was evident.

"Shit," she muttered while swinging her right leg up and over the horse. She hit the soft ground with barely an audible thud. Before setting off to investigate, she secured the horse, leaving enough slack so it could dodge and fight back against an afflicted.

A single one, she thought. God help the beast should more dead arrive. At least she wouldn't be traveling so far she wouldn't hear the horse's calls for help.

But would the others?

She moved from tree to tree. She stopped behind each, waited, listened. Single words could be made out, but nothing that raised a flag.

Raised a flag? Hell, the whole thing did. Turk's bunker had been discreet, yet two days in a row there were people at it.

The field came into view, most of it scorched from the fire. There were ten men, at least, gathered near the opening to the underground entrance. Their banter silenced. Their faces turned grim. She held her breath waiting for what she knew would come next.

And it did.

The first of the dead men was hauled out. Four guys hooked him under his knees and armpits and carried him away. They set him down on a pile of timber and dead grass. The second man emerged. He was lighter. It only took two men to carry him. They dropped him next to the other guy. Their bodies lay distorted on the uneven pile.

A guy carrying a red gas can walked over and began dousing the corpses. He turned the can upright, ensuring every last drop was used. Then he handed it off to a younger guy, maybe around

Jake's age. He kind of reminded her of Jake, too. Same hair color, build.

Her thoughts drifted back to Emma. Were they still at the stables? Maybe she'd made a mistake. Maybe coming back here and seeing this was a sign she should return. She didn't realize she was biting down on her bottom lip until the pain became unbearable.

The man next to the bodies pulled what appeared to be a pack of matches from his pocket. He attempted to strike match after match, but the wind kept blowing them out. He stood there, tapping his foot impatiently, waiting for a couple of guys to come form a shield for him.

That was all it took.

He held the lit match, cupping his hand around it. The guys moved with him toward the soon-to-be funeral pyre. They shuffled around like a herd of elephants.

Then they all stopped.

The guy with the match peered over the shoulders of the men in front of him. One by one they turned, too, all looking in her direction.

Addy leaned back. Somehow the sound didn't register until she heard it a second time.

The horse was neighing fiercely.

She took a few steps back and tripped over a log. Lying on her side, she looked back at the field. About half the men were already crossing it, heading in her direction. Their long rifles were aimed at the ground, or in her general area.

Addison scurried to her knees and began moving. Walking at first. Then picking up the pace. She dodged obstacles, threw her hand around trees, scratching it on the bark, as she used them to change her momentum. Through the woods she saw what was happening.

Afflicted surrounded the horse. The animal bucked and

decapitated one as Addy closed the distance. She stopped, lifted the pistol, and put the nearest in her sights. It didn't matter if the men heard. Hell, it might give them reason to pause.

She unleashed the first round with thunderous effect. The afflicted snapped back and dropped to the ground. Addison didn't hesitate. She put a round through two more, leaving one last afflicted who was too close to the horse for her to fire. She freed her knife from the sheath and crept up behind the afflicted.

The horse watched her approach and stopped stomping on the ground. The afflicted leaned his head back, shrieked in a way Addy hadn't heard before. It echoed louder than the gunshots had sounded at the moment of firing.

The knife slid through the afflicted's neck, past the base of its skull, and into the remnants of its brain. Addison freed the blade, and the dead settled to rest in front of the horse.

She was careful to maneuver around the afflicted on her way to the tree. She sliced the rope instead of untying it. There wasn't time. The men were closing in. Their shouts overtook the silence. Addison threw her left foot into the stirrup and had the horse moving before her ass had touched the saddle.

She hadn't made it twenty feet when she heard one of the men yell to the others.

"There's some stables near here. Bet she's headed there."

Whether it was her stomach that rose into her throat, or her heart that sunk to her stomach, she felt her body start to go limp. Upwards of ten armed men would now be heading to the place where she left Emma.

She clutched the reins tight and tugged them, turning the horse toward the stables.

If the men had transportation, horses or ATVs, they had to run back for them. This gave Addison a sizable lead on them. If they intended to pursue on foot, the stables were still a few miles away.

At best they'd clear each mile through the woods at ten minutes. She would make it in half the time, at worst.

She dug her heels into the horse's ribs. The animal pushed hard, weaving through the trees and hurdling obstacles. Everything went past in a blur. Fear could do that.

Anticipation rose as they hustled over the final distance. She began to wonder if she would find Emma and Jake at the stables.

What if the men were already there? What if they had a car or truck near the field?

Even with her direct route, she couldn't beat a vehicle on the open highway. They'd have to cover some ground off-road, but traveling sixty miles an hour on asphalt rendered that point moot.

She emerged from the woods to find the stables standing. The area surrounding it felt surreal. Impaled afflicted paid her no mind as she hopped off the horse in front of the gate. She had it open and led the horse through within ten seconds, then shut and latched it again. She dropped the reins and ran to the building, calling out Emma's name. The horse trotted close behind her. Even with the barrier, it had no desire to remain in the presence of the dead.

The stable doors flung open. Jake tried to hold Emma back, but she broke free of his grasp and sprinted toward Addison.

"You came back for me," she said as she slammed into Addy. "You came back."

Addison lifted the younger girl up and continued toward the barn. "We have to get moving."

Jake squinted at her as she drew close. "What's going on?"

"I went back to the bunker," she said. "There were more of them. Had to be a dozen. They heard the horse, and one of them mentioned this place."

He hung his head. "Shit."

"Yeah, shit is right. We gotta get moving. Get your horse ready and meet us outside." She set Emma down. "Go grab your things. Hurry."

The girl sprint down the aisle between the stalls and climbed the makeshift ladder to the loft.

Addison turned to Jake, who was pacing in front of the open doors, rubbing his scraggly beard.

"What aren't you telling me?" she said. "Why didn't you mention there were so many others?"

"Didn't think we'd encounter them," he said. "I thought they'd..."

She waited for him to continue, but he stared out toward the field. "You thought they'd what?"

"Go back north." He stepped through the opening. "You hear that?"

"Back north where? And hear what?" She followed him outside. The distant hum grew into a low rumble. "That's them, and they're almost here. We need to get moving."

Addison darted through the opening.

"Go upstairs with the girl. Stay put and let me handle this."

She stopped like a ballplayer caught in a pickle, her front foot sliding on loose hay. She turned back to him. "Do what?"

"Just stay up there!"

"Are you crazy?"

"I can handle this, okay. Let me handle it."

Brakes squealed from somewhere beyond the trees. Doors creaked open, then slammed shut, at least eight of them. Before Jake threw the stable doors shut again, she spotted the first of the men emerging from the woods near the gate.

Addison ran to the ladder and hurried upstairs.

"What is it?" Emma said.

Addy ignored her as she hustled to the opposite end where she opened the window enough to see and hear what happened below. A few moments later she felt Emma's hand on her shoulder.

She reached up with her own and placed it on top of the girl's, giving it a squeeze.

"Is everything okay?" Emma whispered.

"I don't know. I think he's going to give himself up."

"What? Why? We could have escaped."

Addison shook her head. "I don't think so."

A cool wisp of wind blew steady through the small opening. The odor of gasoline rode with it. The trucks idled somewhere not too far away. Five men gathered near the gate. Addison spotted at least three more in the woods. The others had to be close by.

"There gonna be a problem here, son?" one of the men yelled out. Addison couldn't tell which one.

She leaned forward so she could see directly below. Jake held up his hands and said nothing. He was going to do it. Going to give himself up. Why? They could have run for it if he hadn't argued with her.

The gate flung open and the five armed men entered the yard. Addison's pulse quickened, as did her breathing. She considered taking the men out, but doing so would be signing Jake's death warrant. They'd certainly unload on him before she could kill all five. She focused on the group of men too long, and nearly missed four others emerging from the woods.

After they joined the others, it became clear that one man was held in higher regard. He had dark hair, streaked with sliver. His beard was full, like he'd grown it out before the outbreak. When the others stopped, he continued forward a few more steps. Then he stood there, nodding, looking at Jake.

"Put your hands down, son," the guy said.

Jake's arms fell to his side. His shoulders slumped. The older man lifted his hand and gestured for Jake to come to him.

"Don't go," Addy whispered.

"What?" Emma whispered into her ear. Her breath was hot and tickled.

161

Addy shook her head while continuing to watch the scene unfold outside. Jake had started walking toward the older man. He stopped a few feet short. For a few moments, nothing happened. Then the older guy grabbed Jake by the shoulders. He nodded a couple times, said something that couldn't be heard up in the loft.

Addison had trouble processing what occurred next.

The older man pulled Jake in close to him. But it wasn't to hit him or throw him to the ground. He embraced the younger man, holding tight with one arm across Jake's back while lightly slapping his back with the other hand. Jake's body started shaking, like he was crying.

"All right, son," the older man said, louder now. "Brady said he saw two girls, or a woman and a girl. I'm guessing they're inside?"

"It's just me," Jake said as he dragged his sleeve across his face wiping away tears and snot.

But it didn't fool the old guy. His gaze fell upon Addy's. Locked onto her eyes. He nodded, slowly, while gesturing for a couple of his men to head inside the stables.

"Son, just tell me the truth, and nothing'll happen to them."

Jake looked back over his shoulder, up to the loft. He too met Addison's stare. He slammed his eyelids shut before lowering his head again. "They're just trying to get somewhere. Don't get them mixed up with us."

The older man handed Jake off to another, then made his way up to the stables. He stopped in front of the doors and looked up. "Come on down. My men are waiting for you inside. We'll see to it that you're taken care of."

Addy backed away from the opening, out of the finger of light stretching across the floor.

"Should we go?" Emma asked, digging her fingers into Addison's forearm.

"I don't think we have a choice."

"We can fight them." The girl stood tall, chest puffed out. Her father would have been proud.

"We'll die." Addy started toward the ladder. "Stay close to me. We'll see where they take us, and at some point, we'll make our move."

But after they climbed down the ladder, she realized they would've been better off fighting.

TWENTY

SWEAT AS COLD AS ICE TRICKLED DOWN THE SIDE OF SEAN'S forehead until it collided with the curve of his beard. His heart thumped against his ribs. A spreading pain gripped his midsection.

The man across from him sat unflinching and unblinking. No smile or other hint that his question to Sean, *"Do you want to live or die today?"* had been a joke. His hands were out of sight. Maybe he had a pistol mounted under the desk and held it now. Sean's answer would determine how he used it.

Breathe, he told himself. No way they would've wasted water and soap on him if the plan was to shoot him here. Medrick used the question as a test. A way to judge the character of the man across from him. Sean's answer had to stand up to the question. Figuring out what that meant to Medrick posed a problem on its own.

Sean only cared in the context of getting to his daughter, but somewhere deep in his mind, he knew the chances of finding her were slim. Beyond the faint glimmer of hope that he'd find her, he didn't care whether he lived or died. In some ways, Medrick would do him a favor by ending his life today.

"We're all dead," Sean said. "Most of us don't realize it yet."

Sean couldn't see that his answer affected Medrick one way or another. The guy stared at him, unflinching and unblinking, still. After several seconds, he brought his left hand up and rested his wrist on the edge of the desk.

"That's got nothing to do with today, though. Specifically, I want to know if you want to live or die *today*."

"I think you've already made up your mind. Quite frankly, I don't care what happens to me today. I've died a little bit every day for the past eight years, some days more than others. One day, this'll all be over. Until that day comes, I'm gonna keep fighting for God knows what reason. Maybe it's hope that this'll end and things will be normal again."

Medrick chuckled. "Shit ain't never gonna be normal again." He brought his other hand up quickly. Sean flinched. It wasn't much, but he could see by the slight arch in Medrick's brow that he'd noticed. The man made a show of presenting his empty hand, letting it hover in the air over the desk.

The still room remained silent except for a faint ticking coming from the silver watch on the desk. The second hand flicked forward, paused for a tick, and moved again, over and over. When Sean looked up from it, Medrick was watching him.

"What is it you want from me?" Sean asked.

"One of them gnaw on your leg?" Medrick said.

Sean swallowed hard. He didn't want to reveal too much to the man. "I was in the military."

Medrick squinted at him. "Eight years ago?"

Sean nodded, said nothing.

"IED?"

"Friendly fire."

"Damn. Sucks."

"Sure does."

"Why didn't the government give you something better than a toothpick to walk around on?"

Sean tugged on his pant leg, pulling it over his thigh. He lifted his leg and tapped on the titanium connection bonded to his femur.

Medrick leaned over the desk to get a closer look. "Well, what happened to the rest? You hock it for beer money?"

"Shit happens, I guess. Had to make do with what I could find."

Medrick sat back down, grinning, shaking his head. "Someone stole your fucking leg? Man, that is hardcore."

Sean shrugged and said nothing. What was he supposed to say next?

"Yeah, but I got a replacement not too far from here, so if you'll let me borrow one of your SUVs I promise to bring it right back."

No, he had to keep that close to the vest.

Medrick rose, wiping his fingers across his desk as he did so. He frowned as he glanced down at the dust covering his fingertips. Shaking himself back into focus, he pointed at Sean. "Get up. We're going for a walk."

They exited the building, which Sean assumed Medrick used as his private residence. A short walk later, they entered the middle building. The door opened when they were six feet out. Heat enveloped Sean, a sharp contrast to the thirty-degree air they had walked through.

It took a few seconds for Sean's eyes to adjust to the dim entry-way. The doors fell shut behind them, clanking together in a way that left him feeling they were safe from anything outside, but also realizing they wouldn't be easy to open from the inside either.

Medrick's hand slapped the center of Sean's back. It remained there as the other man guided him to the right. They were in a reception area. Blue chairs connected by a steel beam were anchored to the walls in a U-shape. Directly ahead was a chest-high partition. On either side of it were doors. No one sat behind the partition. Mounted to the wall behind the empty stool was a black board with white letters affixed to it. What once probably listed employees now had ridiculous phrases spelled out.

Brains 4 Sale.

Hold My Beer.

Asshats Stay Out.

And others, some of which almost gave Sean a smile. Medrick looked amused as he followed Sean's gaze.

"I guess you'd say some of the guys here are pranksters," he said.

"They're clever," Sean deadpanned.

Medrick tilted his head, puffed out a breath of air. "Yeah, well, whatever. Let's keep moving."

They went through the door on the right. A steady chink-chink sound drummed in the background. Sean looked around the room and couldn't find the source among the still machinery.

"What was this place?" he asked.

Medrick ignored the question as he pushed Sean onward and around the equipment. They came to another heavy door that led to a hallway lined with brown carpet and illuminated by dull fluorescents.

The right side of the hallway was lined with doors every fifteen feet or so. Those rooms were on the perimeter of the building. The left side had far fewer. The manufacturing side.

"Are you making something here?" he said.

Medrick continued to ignore him. He now hummed the theme song to *Gilligan's Island*. How lucky would those bastards have been in this day and age? Wouldn't have to worry about the afflicted on that island.

Sean felt a yank on his shirt and stopped. Medrick stepped ahead of him, holding a finger up.

"Wait here," he said before knocking on a door.

A muffled, "Hold on a second," preceded the door opening an inch or two.

Medrick flashed a toothy grin. "Sup, Doc? Not interrupting, am I?"

The man pushed the door shut, then it sounded as though he were sliding a security chain free from the door. He pulled it open and stood there wearing a white t-shirt and a pair of boxers.

Medrick looked past him, still grinning. "Guess I did interrupt. Sorry, sweetheart, we need the Doc right now more than you."

A few seconds later a woman wrapped in a pink robe emerged and hurried down the hallway past Sean.

Medrick leaned against the doorway, where the man he'd called Doc was standing. "Sharon? Really?"

The other guy shrugged. "Take what you can get these days. Right?"

Medrick's face tightened. He shook his head. "No, I pretty much take what I want." He winked and the smile returned. "Anyway, we're not here to talk about fornicating. I want you to meet my man Sean here."

The guy nodded. "Pendergast is the name, but everyone calls me Doc, on account that I was, wait for it, a doctor before all this shit happened."

Sean returned the nod and said nothing.

Doc turned his attention back to Medrick. "Is he sick?"

"No, well, I don't think so." He looked back at Sean. "You sick?"

"No."

"See, he says no. Made it through initiation without a scratch on him."

"Impressive," Doc said with a quick nod. "So what do you need?"

"Show him your leg, Sean."

Sean hiked up his pant leg, revealing the makeshift prosthetic.

The doctor almost looked pained at the sight of it.

"You got anything better?" Medrick asked.

Doc turned and leaned out of sight for a moment before stepping into the hallway. He held a keyring, not unlike the one possessed by the woman upstairs. "Follow me."

They went further down the hall, with Medrick and Doc walking shoulder to shoulder, Sean behind them. Were they being watched? Seemed odd Medrick would turn his back to him like this. Did he think some kind of trust had been established between them?

Medrick turned to the side and waited for Sean to catch up. He draped his arm across Sean's shoulders as he looked back the way they had come.

"You interested in that fine piece of meat he had in there?" Medrick said. "I can make that happen. Just say the word."

Sean didn't look at the guy. "I'm good."

Medrick grabbed Sean's wrist and jerked it up and down. "I bet you are." He let go. "But seriously, we got plenty like her here."

Sean thought of Beth, wondering where she was right now, and if the woman who'd given birth hours earlier would soon be relegated to prostitute duty.

Doc lifted the keyring over his head and shook it. The keys jangled together. The sound muffled as he sorted through the stack and selected the right one for the door he stopped in front of.

"In here, my friend, is something I think you'll like."

He pushed the door open and waited in the hallway until Medrick started toward the door. Sean followed behind. Doc entered last, shutting and locking the door behind him.

The room was a ten-by-ten square with no window. Was the back wall adjacent to another room? Sean thought about the walk over with the woman. He couldn't recall if there were windows cut into the exterior. The building was blurred in his memory.

The overhead lights were dull yellow fluorescents. A small desk and chair were pushed into the corner. A white laminate calendar was spread across the desk. The days were written in black ink. Several of them circled in red.

Opposite the desk were several boxes stacked along the wall. Were they filled with medical supplies? How had they come across so much stuff? Maybe it had all been here, and these guys had lucked into it. Probably not. Sean figured they'd looted or taken it all by force.

Doc reached up and pulled the top box off the right stack. Then a second. And a third. He pulled the fourth and carried it over to the desk.

Sean knew why they were there, he just didn't believe their words had any merit.

So when the Doc pulled a black and muted grey titanium prosthetic leg from the cardboard box, he couldn't believe what he was seeing.

"Drop your pants," Doc said.

Sean had to blink the guy into focus before the words registered. He complied and took a seat on the desk next to the man. He stared at the prosthetic.

Medrick settled into the chair. He rolled it back toward the door where he could put his feet up on one of the discarded boxes from the pile.

Doc slid the end over Sean's leg, then held out both hands. "Let's see how it measures up."

Sean grabbed the man's hands and slid off the table. The prosthetic hit the ground first, setting his hips off-center. "Just a little off."

Doc slid open a drawer and pulled out a few hardcover books. "Lift your foot."

Sean did and waited for the man to slide a book under. Once he got the signal, he set it back down. "Almost."

The man rooted through the drawer again, coming away with a yellow legal pad. Sean repeated the process.

"I think that's perfect," he said.

"Great," Medrick said. "I saw a movie once where they made this dude taller by breaking his legs and stretching them while the bone regrew."

Sean furrowed his brow, not sure if the man was serious. The grin and laugh that followed was all he had to hear.

"I'm thinking we get the guys to do a little work on this." He pulled the prosthetic away and removed the socket. He measured the height of the book and legal pad, then marked the same distance on a length of steel he could attach at the knee joint and create a hook that would be secured onto Sean's femur attachment.

Medrick rose and slid his chair away from the door. "I'll take that, Doc. You mind keeping Sean here for a little while? Give him a once over and all that good stuff."

Doc nodded as he extended the prosthetic, foot first, to Medrick.

Medrick pulled the door open and stepped into the hallway. Before the door fell shut, he stuck his head back into the room.

"Sean?"

"Yeah?"

"You want to live or die today?"

Sean felt the knot reform in his stomach. He held Medrick's gaze for several seconds before answering. "Live."

Medrick smiled and winked. "Well, hang tight, 'cause I'm gonna give you a chance to prove it in a few hours."

The story continues in Affliction Z: Fractured (Part 2). Coming soon.

Sign up for L.T. Ryan's Affliction Z new release newsletter and be the first to find out when new the next story is published.

As a thank you for signing up, you'll receive a complimentary copy of *The Sickness of Ron Winters: An Affliction Z Short Story.*

To sign up, simply fill out the form on the following page: **http://afflictionz.com/newsletter/**

CLICK here to like Affliction Z on facebook.

ALSO BY L.T. RYAN

Affliction Z Series

Affliction Z: Patient Zero

Affliction Z: Abandoned Hope

Affliction Z: Descended in Blood

Affliction Z Book 4 - Coming Soon

The Jack Noble Series

The Recruit (free)

Noble Beginnings

A Deadly Distance

Ripple Effect (Bear Logan)

Thin Line

Noble Intentions

When Dead in Greece

Noble Retribution

Noble Betrayal

Never Go Home

Beyond Betrayal (Clarissa Abbot)

Noble Judgment

Never Cry Mercy

Deadline

End Game

Mitch Tanner Series

The Depth of Darkness

Into the Darkness

ABOUT THE AUTHOR

L.T. Ryan is a *USA Today* and international bestselling author. The new age of publishing offered L.T. the opportunity to blend his passions for creating, marketing, and technology to reach audiences with his popular Jack Noble series.

Living in central Virginia with his wife, the youngest of his three daughters, and their three dogs, L.T. enjoys staring out his window at the trees and mountains while he should be writing, as well as reading, hiking, running, and playing with gadgets. See what he's up to at http://ltryan.com.

Social Medial Links:

- Facebook (L.T. Ryan): https://www.facebook.com/LTRyanAuthor

- Facebook (Jack Noble Page): https://www.facebook.com/JackNobleBooks/

- Twitter: https://twitter.com/LTRyanWrites

- Goodreads: http://www.goodreads.com/author/show/6151659.L_T_Ryan

Printed in Great Britain
by Amazon

78035282R00109